CRASHED

MASON BROTHERS, BOOK 2

JULIE KRISS

Book 1 of the Mason Brothers Series:

Spite Club

ONE

Andrew

"THIS SUMMER IS GOING to be hot," my brother said.

I flipped the page in my sketchbook and started a new drawing. "Uh huh."

"They say it'll break records." Nick came out of the back bedroom and into the living room. "It's only the first week of July and it's already off the charts. I checked the air conditioner," he said, looking at me. "Looks like it works fine. You won't have a problem."

"Right," I said, putting my pencil to paper. I drew a sandy beach, the sand winding away in perspective. Low, white-capped waves rolling gently in. Palm trees.

"There will be storms and other shit like that," Nick said, dropping onto the sofa across from me. "Power outages maybe."

My pencil put a lounge chair on the beach, an umbrella. "I'll be fine."

"Not if the power goes out. I left an emergency number on

the fridge. Keep your fucking phone charged for the next two weeks while I'm gone."

On the beach chair appeared Lightning Man, the superhero Nick and I wrote about in our comics. That is, Nick wrote the stories and I drew the panels. Lightning Man was wearing a cutoff version of his usual black tights and a sleeveless version of his black superhero shirt. His cape was hanging on a nearby palm tree branch and he had sunglasses on. His arms were laced behind his head and he was grinning.

"You know," I told Nick as I drew, "I *would* keep my phone charged if I was the kind of person who liked talking to people. Which I very much am fucking not."

"Keep it charged," Nick growled in a voice that would intimidate anyone who wasn't his big brother. "I might want to call you."

"To check up on me?" I asked. Lightning Man wasn't alone on this beach. "I'm not helpless without you, asshole. You just think I am. Besides, you shouldn't be calling me while you're on your honeymoon. You're supposed to be there with Evie, remember?"

"Evie will want me to call you," Nick said with pissed-off logic. "Besides, it's my honeymoon. I'll call whoever I want, whenever I want. And you better pick up the fucking phone."

I lowered the drawing pad just enough to look at him. My little brother—my only brother—was sprawled on the sofa in the living room of my small bungalow in suburban Millwood, Michigan, glaring across the room at me. Nick Mason was dark-haired, muscled, and what the women liked to call gorgeous, even wearing ratty old jeans and a T-shirt. Since I looked in the mirror every day, I knew he looked a lot like me, except that I was a few years older, my face was thinner, and my hair was a shade darker. I had muscles in my arms and shoulders that were leaner and tighter than his, and my eyes had darkness behind them born of experience he didn't have. But there was no doubt we were brothers.

From the waist down, of course, we didn't look alike at all. Because I was in a wheelchair and he wasn't.

Seven years I'd been like this, ever since a drunk driving accident when I was twenty-three. My buddy was drunk. So was I. He drove. We crashed.

He died. I lived.

That's all I'm going to say about it.

Nick had been my rock through good and bad for those seven years. But now he was married, happy, and taking his new wife on a two-week honeymoon. And it was giving him stress fits to leave me, which pissed me off and warmed my cold, cold heart in equal measures.

I chose option one. "Would you be happier if you could put me in a kennel?" I asked him.

"Shut up," he replied. "I'm looking out for you. I'll have my phone on in Hawaii. You can text me if you need me. Evie, too."

"I won't be texting you, because I'll probably be interrupting something porny, and I don't need that in my life."

"Jesus, I don't know why I bother," Nick said.

My gaze moved to the window. This was standard conversation for Nick and me. We really did piss each other off, though for some reason it didn't keep us from seeing or talking to each other every day. Some things in life are mysterious.

Two weeks. He's going to be gone for two weeks.

I wasn't panicking.

My non-panic was distracted by the sight of a car pulling into the driveway across the street. Being a pathetic shut-in, I knew that Mrs. Welland, the seventy-year-old lady who'd lived in that house, had died two months ago, so it wasn't her. And she'd lived alone, so this was a stranger.

Mrs. Welland hadn't died in the house itself. She'd passed

out at Safeway, someone had called 911, and she'd never come home.

I was pretty glad that if Mrs. Welland had to go, she hadn't died alone in her house with no one to find her. Because I kept an eye on her without her knowing, and I would have figured it out when she didn't pick up her mail. And then I would have had to call 911. And that seemed way too involved for me.

Mrs. Welland didn't have any family that I knew of, so it was a surprise to see the car. It was a Civic, with no logos for cleaning companies or anything on the sides. I saw a California license plate, and I knew that my security cameras would get a record of the number.

If you're going to rob or murder someone, the worst place you can do it is on my fucking street. I'm always home, I never sleep, and I have a ton of very advanced electronic surveillance.

"Hey, asshole," Nick said from the sofa. "Remember me?"

I looked back at him. He was scowling at me. He and Evie had gotten married at City Hall, which was wheelchair accessible. I'd worn a suit. Our mother came—she'd been out of our lives for a long time, but now she was back. Our father didn't, because no one had invited him. As far as I knew, he hadn't even been told that the wedding happened.

We were a fucked-up family. Nick should go to Hawaii if he wanted to, be happy if he wanted to. He'd dropped out of college when I had my accident and he'd never gone back. I was a selfish asshole. It was only two weeks. I was thirty fucking years old. I could do without him.

"Don't you have a plane to catch?" I asked him.

"Not for a few hours yet."

There was hesitation in his voice, and I hated to hear it. In that moment, I fucking hated it.

"Go," I said. "Go sit on a beach, snorkel in the ocean, climb a volcano. Drink fruity drinks. Get laid. Just go."

I wasn't going to do any of those things. Technically I could drink a fruity drink if I wanted, but that would be pretty lame sitting alone in my house in Michigan. As for getting laid, even though the equipment worked just fine, there was no chance in hell. To get laid you generally have to leave the house and have a working body. You also have to have a personality that even slightly attracts women. All of which crossed me out.

I couldn't do those things, but Nick could.

"Go," I said again. "I'll be fine."

He reluctantly got off the couch, found his baseball cap, and put it on. "The schedule is on the fridge, with the phone numbers," he said.

"Yes, Mom."

"I'll call you later, asshole," he said, and I heard the door close behind him.

I tried not to feel the hollowness in my chest, the tightness in my throat at the sound. I just sat there and took one breath, and then another. That was how I got through a lot of the harder things. One breath after another. If you can take one breath, then you can take another and another after that. If that's all you can do, then you do it.

I looked out the window again. Nick's car pulled out of the driveway and drove off. The Civic was still across the street.

As I watched, the driver's door opened and a woman got out. She had blonde hair cut just below her chin. She was wearing jeans, a tight black T-shirt, and flip-flops. when she closed the door and turned, I saw a long sweep of bangs falling over her forehead to her cheekbones and big, dark sunglasses that took up half her face, movie-star style. Below the sunglasses, her nose was perfect and her lips were full and glossy. The T-shirt said *Get the fuck out of my business* in bold white letters.

She hitched a purse up on her shoulder and slammed the car door like she owned the whole block. She glanced up and down the street and then tilted her head back in a *kill me now* dramatic gesture. Then she rounded the car, walked to the door of Mrs. Welland's house, opened it with a key from her purse, and was gone.

I watched for a while longer, but she didn't come out again.

Had she bought the house? It hadn't been listed for sale; it was too soon. Or was she an inside buyer?

If she wasn't, then who the hell was she?

TWO

Andrew

IT WAS none of my business. And it didn't even matter. I didn't know any of my neighbors because I never left my house. I wouldn't know this one either.

I moved my hands to wheel away from the window and realized I still had the sketch pad in my lap. It had the unfinished drawing of Lightning Man on the beach, grinning in his lounge chair with his hands locked behind his head. I'd started the outline of a woman standing next to him—I'd planned to draw Judy Gravity, the heroine of the comics, who was brainy and wore dark-framed glasses. Judy was a bit uptight, so from time to time I'd draw her naked or scantily clad just to amuse myself. It always got a rise out of Nick when I did it. I'd planned to draw Judy standing next to Lightning Man's chaise, about to take her bikini top off, as a goodbye present to Nick, but I'd gotten distracted and he'd left before I could finish it.

Now I looked at the drawing and pictured a different woman

instead. A real one instead of the made-up Judy. One with bobbed blonde hair, sunglasses, pouting lips, and attitude.

Desperate much, Mason?

I put the sketch pad aside and wheeled to the bank of computer monitors I had set up in my living room. Even though Nick and I were independently wealthy—our parents' trust funds saw to that—I'd worked for years as a freelance computer programmer. I was good at it, it was something I could do from home, and it kept me busy.

Lately I'd been turning down programming work to draw the Lightning Man comics more and more. Nick and I had a Lightning Man website now, where we sold downloads of all the issues as well as print copies. It had started small, but every month we saw more and more downloads. It was pretty fucking awesome, seeing readers enjoy something you made. It was much better than spending my days dry-eyed, staring at PHP.

Nick had left a bunch of potential stories in our shared online file, and while he was away I may as well start drawing. But first I switched on one of the side monitors to show the feed from one of my front-of-house cameras. This was the one I'd originally set up so I could keep an eye on the house across the street, just in case Mrs. Welland fell down her front steps or her mail started ominously piling up. After Mrs. Welland died, there was no need to monitor that feed anymore—until now.

I started drawing, and half an hour later the dark-haired woman came out of the house again. She opened the Civic's hatchback, leaned all the way in—her ass was perfect in those jeans—and came out with two duffel bags, then some boxes, and finally a couple of black garbage bags. So she was moving in, then, at least for a while. But she didn't have much stuff—no furniture, no moving van. Just her little car.

Who moved all the way from California with only a few bags and boxes?

Who was she?

None of your business.

I turned off the camera feed and went back to work.

I LASTED UNTIL MIDNIGHT. Lying in bed, in the dark and the quiet, my work done and my meds taken, I finally gave in.

I sat up and pulled out my laptop, woke it up. Most people would have difficulty finding out who their new neighbor was. Not me. I logged into a few different sites I knew, typed in a few lines of code, ran some queries.

You could just introduce yourself and ask her name, like a normal person.

I snorted to myself. It wasn't going to happen. I didn't do small talk. I didn't do polite introductions, especially to gorgeous women. Hell, I didn't even do anything that required me to wheel out the front door, even though the doorway and the front ramp were modified so that I could. This was what I did: learn things I wasn't supposed to know, late at night so I could avoid lying alone in the dark.

I hated the dark.

That wasn't a fact I shared with anyone. Not even my therapist. But I had my worst anxiety attacks in the dark, my deepest depressions. The dark was when the things I fought every day came out and won.

So instead of thinking about the dark, I looked up my neighbor.

It was easy because of the Civic, of course. There were a dozen ways I could have found her, but a basic hack into the DMV database with the make, model, and license plate gave me everything I wanted to know.

Her name was Tessa Hartigan. She was twenty-seven. Her

permanent address was in California, so either she was visiting or she hadn't changed her address yet. Judging by her luggage, it could be either one.

I could have stopped there, but I didn't. I opened another browser and did a Google search. She had no Facebook account, no social media at all except Instagram. The avatar was her face, and the description said *Model. Sagittarius. Chocolate chip cookie lover. Contact me for bookings!*

A model? I clicked into her feed.

And froze.

Oh, sweet Jesus.

There was my neighbor, posed with her hands on her hips, a pleasant smile on her face. She had sheer pink lipstick on and darkly made-up eyes. Her blonde bob was tucked behind her ears. She was wearing black lace panties, a black lace bra, and nothing else.

The caption said, *Check out the sexy winter line from LoveIt Lingerie in LA! Link in my bio!*

The next photo was from the same shoot, except the bra and panties were hot pink. Tessa Hartigan had only one hand on her hip and she was laughing. The caption said, *Outtake from yesterday's shoot. We had so much fun!*

There were more. Lots more. The shots weren't erotic—they were catalog shots, meant to sell a product.

My new neighbor was a lingerie model.

"Great," I said out loud to no one, my voice a croak. "That's just fucking great."

Instead of the elderly Mrs. Welland, I now had a hot-as-fuck woman living across the street. One who took most of her clothes off for a living. One who I could look at in lingerie anytime I wanted to.

And all I could feel was panic. My blood pounded in my head, inside my ears. My throat was dry. *She's none of your busi-*

ness, the voice in my head said. *She'll never come near you. Never talk to you. You'll never have a fucking thing to do with her, and you know it.*

I clicked the browser with Instagram closed. Then I clicked into the database sites and logged out, closed them too.

My hands were icy. I closed my laptop, put it on the bedside table. "None of my fucking business," I said aloud, to no one. Because I was alone.

I picked up my phone and swiped through my security apps. I controlled the lights, the locks, and all the appliances in my house through the dashboard, and I checked to make sure everything was as it should be. Then I clicked to turn out the bedroom lights. I put the phone down and lay back in the dark.

I closed my eyes and saw Tessa Hartigan in the pink lingerie on the backs of my eyelids. Then in the black lingerie.

"Fuck," I said aloud.

It was a long time before I fell asleep.

THREE

Tessa

"NANCY," I said, "I'm begging you. You have to help me. I'm stuck in goddamned Michigan."

On the other end of the phone, my agent laughed. "Well, I told you," she said. "You should have stayed in L.A."

I sighed. I was in my bedroom, still wet from the shower and wearing a bathrobe. I fiddled with the thermostat, trying to make it go colder. It was hot in here. "What was I supposed to do?" I said. "My grandmother died and left me a house. A *free* house. What would you do if you were given a free house?"

"Me?" Nancy said. "Probably sell it and use the money to buy Fendi bags. Anything other than moving to Michigan."

"I thought it would be nice to live in a house for once," I said, poking the thermostat again. "I have more than one room to myself here instead of living with roommates in a shitty L.A. apartment. There are lawns here. Sprinklers. Kids on bikes, if you can believe it. There's almost no smog and nothing's on fire."

"Jesus, it sounds fucking awful."

I didn't have the heart to tell her that the most popular place to eat in my neighborhood was the Cheesecake Factory, and that literally nothing was gluten-free. "It's been five days, and I'm climbing the walls," I said, getting down to business. "I need work."

"Honey," Nancy said, "the lingerie business isn't exactly centered in Butt-Fuck Michigan. You knew that when you left."

I gave up on the thermostat. It was ten o'clock in the morning, it was already hot outside, and it wasn't much cooler in here. Every room in this house was hot. I'd barely slept for days. "There are catalogs east of Colorado. I know there are. Someone, somewhere, must want a bra modeled. That person needs me."

"I know, babe. You can sell bras all day every day and twice on Sunday. But work isn't thick on the ground. You might have to get a day job."

This had already crossed my mind. Like just about everyone else in L.A., I had done plenty of bartending and waiting tables while I waited for my big modeling break. I was a walking cliché. "I know. And I will. But I need you to find me *real* work."

"The fact is, I don't really do long distance," Nancy said. "I told you that at our goodbye dinner before you left."

Had she? We'd both been drunk. Or at least I had. Nancy was only a few years older than me, and she was slim and gorgeous. Why she wasn't a model herself, I had no idea. But she was a killer agent, and I'd been happy to land her. "I don't remember you saying anything like that."

"I did. After the margaritas and before the gin. I love you, gorgeous, but business is business. You know how it goes."

I stood paused in the middle of my grandma's suburban bedroom, sweating in the heat, surrounded by dated furniture and flowery window treatments. "Are you... Are you dumping me?" I asked her.

"Not dumping," she corrected me. "I'm staying in alignment with my goals. My goals being to have working clients who make me money. You don't fit those goals anymore, honey, so I have to realign."

She didn't even sound sorry. We'd worked together for three years. I scrubbed a hand through my damp hair. "What about my goals?"

"Well, what are they?" Nancy asked me reasonably. "If your goal was a modeling career, then leaving L.A. was not in alignment. Perhaps you should re-center and reconnect with your inner self."

"And in the meantime, don't call you."

"You know it isn't personal." As if on cue, there was a beep on the line. "That's my new girl. She says she's Giselle's second cousin, but I think she's lying. I have to go."

I hung up and tossed the phone on the bed. Looked around.

I hadn't known my grandmother. My mother called herself a "free spirit"—basically, she was a hippie. She'd met my father and gotten pregnant at nineteen. The two of them had packed a van and driven away from Michigan forever, on a quest to find themselves. They'd left my grandmother behind and never brought me back.

Now it was twenty-seven years later. My parents hadn't worked out, of course. Mom was in Colorado, and Dad was in Texas of all places, where he ran an incense shop and lived with a different hippie woman—one much younger than he was. And I'd drifted to L.A., where I was hoping to make it as a model.

I wasn't the best-looking woman in L.A. I wasn't the sexiest, or the skinniest, or—this one hurt—the most talented. In high school in Colorado, I'd been pretty. In the sea of gorgeous people in Los Angeles, I was nothing much. I'd lived in a series of apartments not much bigger than this bedroom, with roommates who sometimes creeped me out, working occasional bar jobs and going on auditions. I'd gone to L.A. out of desperation, thinking I could be free of my shitty life in Colorado, where I had nearly crashed and burned. I'd resurrected myself and run. And it had been fun, for a while.

At least, I thought it had. But the years had ground by one after another, and my career had gone nowhere. Neither had my love life, because L.A. was full of narcissistic jerks. In a way, I was just existing, and I didn't know what to do about it. Most of the time it didn't feel like anything much was wrong, but that was because I was intentionally numb.

Then my grandmother died and I found out she'd left her house to me. She was still mad at Mom, so she'd cut her out of the will—everything she had skipped a generation and went to me.

And I hadn't thought twice. I'd taken it. I'd packed my bags and left without a backward glance.

If your goal was a modeling career, then leaving L.A. was not in alignment. Perhaps you should re-center and reconnect with your inner self.

Nancy was heartless, and she was full of L.A. bullshit-speak, but part of me wondered if she had a point.

I sighed and dropped my robe. It was time to see if the Cheesecake Factory was hiring.

FOUR

Tessa

"MILLWOOD ISN'T SO BAD," the woman from down the street said. "I mean, we're not rich, so we're not assholes."

We were standing in my driveway. I'd been about to get into my car and drive to the nearest batch of big box stores and chain restaurants to apply for jobs when these two women had walked by. They were in their mid-thirties, both wearing capri-length yoga pants and tank tops, their hair tied up in ponytails. In L.A., these women would be wearing $500 yoga outfits and weigh around ninety-five pounds. In Michigan the outfits were Walmart and the number on the scale was higher, but it turned out they were both pretty cool.

"This neighborhood is nice," the woman named Amy said. "There are a lot of older people that have been here for years. And then some of them have started to pass away, like your grandmother. So then you have the younger people, like us."

"I'm around the corner that way," the other woman, Jan, said.

"Amy is four doors down from me. We like to take our walk after we drop the kids at day care."

"I organize the community barbecues," Amy said. She was mixed race, with big brown eyes and a nice Meghan Markle look. "You missed the Fourth of July one, but there's another one in a few weeks. You can meet everyone there."

I pushed my sunglasses higher on my nose. I was sweating under my tank top. "Community barbecue, huh? I'm not sure I'm into those."

Jan looked me up and down, not unkindly. "I guess they don't have those in L.A. You should try it, though."

"What about that house?" I said, nodding to the house across the street. I'd noticed it before—a place with a ramp on the front porch to accommodate a wheelchair. "Who lives there? One of the old people?"

Amy and Jan traded a look, and then they both laughed.

"What?" I said.

"Andrew Mason lives there," Jan said. "He isn't old. He's maybe thirty."

"Oh, shit. And he's in a wheelchair?"

"A drunk driving accident a few years ago," Amy said, more seriously. "Left his legs paralyzed. It split the family apart, too. It created some kind of falling-out with the parents. He moved into that house alone, and he's been there ever since. He almost never leaves."

I looked at the house again. It was tidy, well-kept. The blinds were closed. There was no car in the driveway. But still, I got the feeling that someone was watching. I was probably just being paranoid.

"That's sad," I said. "A young guy getting paralyzed like that. I feel bad for him."

"We all do," Jan said, "and then he always goes and wrecks it."

I looked at her, feeling my eyebrows go up.

"Andrew Mason isn't much of a neighbor," Amy explained. "When he moved in, we tried dropping off welcome gifts. Flowers and whatnot. He never answered the door, and we'd find the gifts jammed into the garbage can at the foot of the driveway."

"He *never* comes to the community barbecues," Jan said.

"Halloween is the worst," Amy said. "We have a lot of kids in this neighborhood, and Halloween is a big thing. Everyone gets into it, but not him. He actually puts a sign up in his window that says *KIDS FUCK OFF.*"

I couldn't help it—I laughed.

"You can laugh, but people get mad when their kids see that kind of language," Amy said primly. "The Masons are some of the richest people in Millwood, so he has plenty of money. But does he give to the annual neighborhood charity drive? No, he doesn't."

"And we can't hate him, because we feel sorry for him," Jan said. "Also, because he's good-looking."

Now my eyebrows rose even higher. "Good-looking?"

The women exchanged another look. "Google him, you'll see," Jan said. "My sixteen-year-old daughter saw him in person once, sitting on his porch. Her exact words were—and I quote —'The legs don't matter, Mom, because he's total swoon.'"

I looked back and forth between the two women. "You're saying that my neighbor across the street is rich, single, good-looking, in a wheelchair, and an asshole?" He sounded like he was very messed up. Messed-up people were the only kind of people who interested me, the only kind of people I understood. "Maybe I'll pay him a visit."

"Yeah, good luck with that." Amy shook her head. "He won't answer the door. He hasn't answered it in the seven years he's lived here."

She was probably right. But the idea stayed in my head as I

drove to the nearest bars and restaurants, filling out applications. It stayed with me as every male manager I met let his eyes crawl up and down me like he had a right to it. It stayed with me as I sat in front of my laptop in my pajamas that evening, unable to sleep in the heat, looking up local modeling agencies who might find me some catalog work.

I got myself a bowl of fat-free ice cream from the freezer, peeking out the window on my way back to my grandmother's sofa. The house across the street was dark except for a single light behind one of the blinds. Nothing moved.

Picking up my laptop again, I downed a bite of ice cream and opened my browser. I Googled *Andrew Mason Millwood Michigan.*

The results came up right away. There were articles about the accident from local papers, because as Amy had said, Andrew Mason's parents were well known in town. There was a photo of a handsome, smooth-cheeked teenager with dark hair, smiling at the camera with the caption *Andrew Mason was known as a talented young man with a lifetime of success ahead of him.*

Was. As if he was dead.

There was a photo of the accident site—a car smashed and twisted around a guardrail, so damaged I was amazed anyone had survived. I felt a little sick. The article said that the driver, Andrew's friend, had died on impact.

My heart heavy, I scrolled to the next photo. It was one of those local-interest anniversary pieces: *Five years on, accident still haunts the Mason family.* The photo showed a man wheeling his chair out of the front doors of a hospital, his face angled away as if he wasn't aware he was being photographed. He was dark-haired with a scruff of beard on his jaw—the same face from the teenaged photo, but this was a man's face, one that knew hardship and sadness. His eyes were set under slashes of brows, his cheekbones sharp as blades. He was wearing a plaid button-down shirt over a muscled set of shoulders and a broad chest. He was deeply, darkly handsome and mysterious, tragic and giving off a vital energy at the same time.

The article said that Mason's parents were divorcing, citing "irreconcilable differences."

I stared at the picture for a long time, alone in my grandmother's living room, eating my fat-free ice cream. I memorized his features, the line of his shoulders. And I decided for myself: This guy was fucking badass.

He was obviously very, very screwed up. Who wouldn't be? Maybe he was almost as screwed up as me.

I wanted to meet him.

It wouldn't be easy.

I started to form a plan.

FIVE

Andrew

I LIVED ALONE, but there was always someone in my house. Grocery delivery; cleaning service; pharmacy delivery; medical visits; landscaping. Even my therapist made house calls. The only good thing about my shitty life was that I had lots and lots of money, so I could make people come to me.

If I didn't have to shop and clean, then what did I do all day? Here's something they don't tell you: when your legs don't work, everything takes longer to do. Getting out of bed, taking a shower, dressing—that shit can take an hour and a half, easy. I had fitted one of the spare bedrooms into a workout room with weights, pulleys, and bars—that took an hour again, and I couldn't skip it because my upper body strength was all I had.

Once I made a cup of coffee and fried an egg, it was halfway to noon. I powered up my monitors, my computer, my server, and got to work.

I could have opened my camera feeds and looked at the house

across the street, but I didn't. Tessa Hartigan and her lacy underwear were none of my business, and I sure as hell wasn't going to start creeping on her like the desperate asshole I was. There was no point to it. She'd never come over here, and I sure as hell would never go over there. End of story.

Today was physiotherapy day, and an hour later the doorbell buzzed. I turned on the security feed. Jon Chu was at my front door camera, wearing his scrubs and waving. I let him in.

"Hot out there!" he said as he walked in. "Supposed to be a heat wave coming."

"Sure," I said, still typing.

He tapped my shoulder. "Let's get moving, Bubble Boy. I get paid by the hour."

I pulled away from my computers, but I took my phone with me. I wheeled after Jon into my exercise room, where he unfolded the table he kept there and helped me on.

"Lower back today," he said.

"Thank fucking God," I replied, pulling off my shirt.

Together we arranged me on my stomach on the table. Jon took a towel and wrapped the waist of my sweatpants with it, jerking them halfway down my ass. Then he took his oil out of his bag.

Anyone who thinks this is awkward has never been in the kind of pain I have. Jon had been my regular physio guy for over a year, and he was magic. I didn't give a shit about having a man's hands on me as long as he took the pain away. I'd been through much, much worse humiliation in my life.

"So Nick is gone on his honeymoon?" Jon asked as he got started.

I grunted as he hit a knot of pain in my lower back. Sitting in a wheelchair is hell on the back muscles, from the neck all the way down. "Two weeks."

"Sucks, man."

"It's fine." It wasn't fine.

He talked like he always did—about a date he'd been on, about his trip to his mother's house for her great cooking. Jon liked to talk without requiring me to say much in return. It made me feel less lonely and at the same time he never pried.

"You working your back muscles lately?" he asked.

I pulled out my phone and tapped it on, swiping through my apps. I called up my security feed, my fingers moving of their own accord. "Trying to."

"Nice job." He whistled. "Wow. Who's that?"

Shit. I hadn't been able to resist it: I'd called up the view of the house across the street. Tessa Hartigan had come out her front door and was unwinding a hose to water her lawn.

"She just moved in," I said, trying to sound casual. Trying to sound like I wasn't spying on her.

"Holy shit." Jon leaned forward, looking more closely at her over my shoulder. "That girl is hot. What's her name?"

"I don't know," I lied.

"But you're one of those computer hacker guys. You could find out, easy."

I already had. "Maybe."

He paused in his work and we both watched her turn on the hose, then stand in the front yard, spraying the grass. Her neck was smooth and white below the ends of her hair. She had her big sunglasses on again, only her perfect nose and pouty lips visible. She was wearing a spaghetti-strap tank top and short shorts. Even her flip-flops were sexy. Jesus Christ.

"You should talk to her," Jon said.

"No I shouldn't." I was mad that he'd caught me creeping on Tessa Hartigan like I couldn't help it. I bit back my anger.

"Sure you should. I keep telling you, women would go crazy for you if you left the house."

"Did you forget the part about my legs?"

"Aw, man, that doesn't matter. As long as the plumbing works."

I glanced over my shoulder at him. "This finally got weird, considering I'm partly naked."

Jon shrugged. "I don't play for your team, man." He pointed to my phone, where my neighbor was spraying water like a cheesy music video. "I play for *that* team."

"Thanks for the insight. My lower back, okay?"

He got back to work, taking his heated towel out of his bag and putting it on me while he worked. It was my lower back—my lumbar spine—that was damaged in the accident, the nerve damage shorting the signal from my brain to my legs. One stupid decision, and my legs weren't getting the message anymore. They probably never would again. I couldn't see the scars from the emergency surgery on my spine, but I knew they were there.

I closed the security app. I didn't want to look at my neighbor anymore.

But Jon wasn't ready to drop the subject. "I think you're too hard on yourself, dude. Another patient of mine, he's in a wheelchair, too. He's on Tinder. I'm telling you, that guy *cleans up*."

"Curiosity fucks," I said. "I'm not interested."

"No way. He's just a player, the same as any guy with legs. Don't you know what year it is? No stigma."

"Trust me, there's stigma."

He sighed. "It's mindset, man. Just mindset. Deep down you know it's true." He took the towel off. "Okay, we're done."

After he left, I grabbed some almonds and orange juice from the fridge and wheeled back to the living room. My phone rang. It was Nick.

I swiped to answer. "I'm answering the phone," I said to my brother without bothering with *hello*. "Are you happy? Can I go back to my life now?"

"What's going on there, fuckface?" Nick said back. "Everything okay?"

"Everything's great. I have hookers here. I'm snorting blow. Just a regular Wednesday at my house."

He ignored me. "Did Jon come for the physiotherapy? I put it on the schedule on the fridge."

"Jesus." I swigged orange juice. "Yes, he did. Everything's fine."

"Donna is supposed to come tomorrow."

I winced. Donna was a "wellness therapist"—that was what she called herself, probably because she wasn't any kind of legit doctor. She'd been hired by my mother.

Two years ago, when my parents divorced, my mother had decided to come back into my life. Nick's, too. She'd apologized for abandoning us after the accident and she'd tried hard to make amends. Part of those amends, in my mother's mind, was hiring Donna to give me her wellness therapy.

Overall, I was good with having my mother back. It sure as hell beat the years when I thought she didn't give a shit about me. But Donna and her wellness therapy were a pain in the ass.

"Aren't you in Hawaii?" I asked my brother. "Why are you fussing about my schedule?"

"Just making sure you're following it," Nick said. "And yes, I'm in fucking Hawaii. It's nice here. You should come sometime."

"What color is the sky in your world?" I swigged more juice. "Kiss Evie for me. Then again, don't, because you'll only remind her that she married the wrong guy."

This was a common line of ribbing with Nick and me. I didn't actually have a thing for Evie, even though she was a hot, curvy redhead, definitely the best-looking woman who had ever been inside my house. Nick and Evie were made for each other. And I didn't have a thing for any woman, because it wasn't going to happen.

I thought of Tessa Hartigan, then pushed the thought away.

There was a muffled female voice on the other end of the phone. Then Nick saying, "No, I'm not telling him that." Then more talking.

"I'm getting old here," I reminded my brother.

Nick sighed. "Evie wants me to say that she loves you."

I put my glass down. For a second I couldn't breathe. Fucking Evie. Neither of us deserved her.

"Well of course she does," I said through the lump in my throat, making my voice sound casual. "Everyone knows I'm the better brother." I cleared my throat. "With the bigger dick."

"I'm not telling her that."

In the beat of silence, my doorbell rang.

"What the fuck was that?" Nick said.

I was frozen in surprise. I wasn't expecting anyone; I had no appointments, no deliveries. No one was supposed to be at my door.

"Andrew?" Nick said.

"It would seem to be my doorbell," I said, wheeling myself over to my monitor and tapping it awake. "Probably just kids." I looked at the front door feed and went very still.

"Well?" Nick said after a minute.

"It's nothing," I managed. "I'll call you later." I hung up.

And looked at the front door feed again.

Tessa Hartigan was standing on my front porch. She was still wearing the spaghetti-strap top and short shorts from before. Her sunglasses were perched on top of her head. She had noticed the camera and had centered herself in front of it, waving.

She carried a white square cake, which she tilted toward the camera. There was one word iced onto the cake:

Hi.

SIX

Tessa

IT HAD BEEN a stroke of genius, really. I'd noticed a bakery in the plaza next to one of the restaurants where I'd applied. I had the feeling that to impress Andrew Mason, I'd have to do something unexpected. A *Hi* cake seemed like just the thing.

But I stood on the porch in dead silence, holding the cake toward the camera over the door and waving. And nothing happened.

"Hey," I said out loud in case he could hear me. "I'm your new neighbor. Come on." I pointed. "Cake here."

Still nothing.

He was home; I knew he was home, because I'd seen a car come and go, an Asian guy in scrubs come to the front door and get let in. Andrew Mason was here, but he was ignoring me.

"Hey," I said again as sweat rolled down my back. Jesus, it was hot. I thought California was hot. Why didn't anyone warn me that Michigan was fucking boiling?

I sighed as sweat rolled down my temples in the silence. Why was I doing this? Why was I going to so much trouble? It wasn't because I thought that poor, sad Andrew Mason needed a friend. It wasn't because I was a naturally kind person. I couldn't have said why I was doing it, in fact. And so far, I wasn't getting anywhere.

And for another reason I couldn't explain, that didn't discourage me. It only made me more determined to get him to answer the goddamn door.

I was wondering what to do—the cake was about to start melting—when my phone pinged in my pocket. An incoming text. I should probably ignore it.

My phone pinged again.

Sighing in annoyance, I balanced the cake on one hand and fished out my phone with the other. Swiped it on. Saw two texts from a number I didn't recognize.

Go away.

I mean it.

I felt my jaw drop. Surprise, first, and then outrage. What the fuck? I immediately hit the button to dial the unknown number.

On the other end, the phone rang once and then a masculine voice said, "Can't you read?"

"Andrew Mason?" I said.

"No, it's Chris Evans. Who the fuck do you think is telling you to go away?"

"How... How the hell did you get my phone number?"

"You have no idea how much personal information the average cell phone transmits. It's all there. It's only a matter of accessing it."

God, what a voice. Deep, even, perfectly calm. And all those big words. I felt a shiver despite my outrage. I couldn't remember the last time a man had given me a shiver.

"So what else do you know about me?" I asked him.

"Your name is Tessa Hartigan, this is your phone number, you have an L.A. address, you're staying in the house across the street," Andrew said. "And you're currently standing on my front porch with a cake that says *Hi* on it for reasons I have yet to understand."

"I'm being neighborly!" I said, exasperated.

"No, you're treating me as an object of pity. That's an entirely different thing."

"You're not an object of pity!" I was shouting now, which I was vaguely aware of, though I didn't really care. "You're my new neighbor, and I'm saying hello! It's what normal people do!"

"How many of your other neighbors did you bring a cake to?"

I was silent, my mouth still open in outrage.

"I thought so," Andrew said. "You can go now. I'm not letting you in."

"Jesus, are you this hard on everyone you meet?" I said, my voice strangled because I was so pissed off.

"Absolutely," he replied. "My therapist tells me it's a defense mechanism. It's a good theory, though when I think it over I find I don't give a fuck."

The cake wobbled in my hand, and I struggled to balance it. The outrage was at war with the shivers again. "I'm glad you have a therapist, because it sounds like you really need it."

"You should know. I'm not the one standing on a stranger's porch in hundred-degree-heat. Besides, I think my therapist is wrong. My problem isn't defensive mechanisms, it's that I hate everyone."

"Including me?"

"The jury's out, but the statistical probability is yes. I'd say sorry, but I don't have any feelings."

"Oh, my God," I said. "This is *cake*. No one hates cake."

"Try me," Andrew Mason said, and hung up.

I stood frozen, the phone still against my ear. Then I put it back in my pocket.

"Fuck you," I muttered darkly. I didn't know if he could hear me, and I didn't care. "You think I don't know assholes? I'm from L.A., jerk. It's an entire city of assholes." I marched to the front door and laid the cake in front of it. "Here's your cake, Andrew Mason. You want to get rid of it, come get it yourself."

The icing was definitely turning liquid in the heat, a few drops running down the sides. In an hour, the *Hi* would be nothing but smears of color, unintelligible. It would be a mess, and the flies and wasps would have a heyday. Too bad.

I turned and walked back across the street to my grandmother's house, my sandals slapping against the hot concrete. When I put the key in the lock, I heard a soft *click* behind me. I turned around to see the front door of Andrew Mason's house clicking shut.

The cake on the porch was gone.

SEVEN

The next morning

TESSA: Well? How was the Hi cake? Admit you ate it.

Andrew: Who is this?

Tessa: Ha ha. You talk tough, but it took you thirty seconds to swoop in and pick it up, big guy.

Andrew: I didn't want flies on my porch, that's all.

Tessa: Sure. It wasn't my sweet cake or my nice icing.

Andrew: I'm not commenting on your icing.

Tessa: Are you flirting with me?

Andrew: Since I said I'm not commenting, no I'm not.

Tessa: It's okay if you flirt. That's what normal single people sometimes do.

Andrew: So you brought me a cake because I'm single?

Tessa: I don't know. Maybe? I brought you a cake because you're the most interesting person on this street. Everyone sort of love-hates you. I wanted to see you for myself.

Andrew: I'm not sure if I should be flattered. I'm deciding no.

Tessa: Do you really put up a sign telling kids to fuck off on Halloween?

Andrew: Since they like to ring my doorbell and run away like I'm Boo Radley, absolutely fucking yes.

Tessa: Are you kidding me??? They made it sound like you're a monster. Their kids need a hard kick in the ass. This year, I'll help you put the sign up myself.

Andrew: So it's my mystique with the neighbors that made you bring me a Hi cake.

Tessa: There's also the fact that you're single and hot. I admit it.

Andrew: Jesus, you need your head examined. Are you one of those crazy needy people who become stalkers?

Tessa: No, I'm just a single girl who spent too many years in L.A. dating a lot of creeps. I like single, hot, interesting guys. So sue me.

Andrew: Why are you in Millwood?

Tessa: My grandmother died and left me a free house. It was better than what I was doing, so I took it.

Andrew: Not a bad deal, I suppose.

Tessa: No, except that I'm starting to think the air conditioning is broken. It's too hot to sleep at night. I'm so fucking tired. You don't know anything about fixing air conditioners, do you?

Andrew: I draw comics. I don't fix things.

Tessa: You draw comics? How did I not know this?

Andrew: Because we literally don't know each other?

Tessa: You ate my cake. We know each other well enough.

Andrew: I find you confusing. What do you want from me?

Tessa: Admit you liked my cake.

Andrew: No.

Tessa: Admit it.

Andrew: My wellness therapist is here. I have to go.

Tessa: Your what?

Andrew: It's fucking weird, so don't ask.

Tessa: Who is that woman getting out of her car in your driveway? Is she actually wearing a caftan?

Andrew: Welcome to my shitty life. Now go away.

Andrew

DONNA THE WELLNESS therapist was about fifty, with drawn-on eyebrows and a large bushel of brown curly hair. She tended to wear caftans over flowered tights, and her bracelets jangled as she motioned with her hands. I told myself the reason I didn't kick her out every time was because my mother had hired her, but the truth was she sort of amused me.

Today she sat facing me where I sat on the couch. I had my legs arranged neatly and carefully, because without any sensation it was easy to injure my legs and ankles without knowing it. But once arranged I lounged back, my plate with its piece of Hi cake in hand.

"So," Donna said after she had closed the blinds and lit some incense, her usual method of starting therapy. "Your brother is gone on his honeymoon. I sense grief coming from you."

"There's no grief," I said, taking a bite. The cake was vanilla, buttery, and—I could admit it to myself—delicious.

"There is definitely grief," Donna said. "It's coming off you as an aura. Deep blue."

"That's just my usual misery," I said. "My grief is burgundy."

She shook her head. The problem with Donna was that it was nearly impossible to tease her. "No, your deep blue is definitely grief. Your brother was very important to you. He was your connection to the outside world."

"Is," I corrected her. "He is my connection, not was."

"But he's married now," she pointed out. "He's found his union with another. That leaves you alone. The honeymoon only outlines what you know deep down is true."

"Is this supposed to be helpful?" I stabbed my fork into my cake.

"When you approach enlightenment, you approach joy," Donna said.

I shrugged. "I have Effexor for that."

Her lips pressed together. "Pharmaceuticals are not the answer."

"Yes, they are. Believe me, they are."

Donna looked at me for a moment, then leaned back in her chair. "I placed some healing crystals around your house last time, but I don't think they've taken effect. I may have to introduce herbs."

I took another bite of cake and watched her think it over. "Why do you bother with me?" I asked after a minute. "I know my mother pays your fee, but that can't be the only reason."

"You're a difficult case, but you're not an impossible one. The spiritual journey is not an easy one, Andrew. It's especially difficult after physical trauma like you've had, which dissociates the body and the spirit. If you wish to commune wholly with yourself, you must make a supreme effort."

"I commune wholly with myself every day in the shower."

Donna waved her hands, jangling her bracelets. "Hostility. Couched in sexual jokes, no less. That means your sexual energies are blocked."

Well, she was dead on about that one. I put down my empty plate. "Maybe," I said.

"So you admit your sexual energies are frustrated." She sat forward.

Seven years. It had been seven fucking years. "A little."

"We are sexual beings, Andrew. Sexuality is part of the wholeness of existence. It must be embraced if we wish our souls to be healthy. As I say, your physical trauma has dissociated that." She waved her hands again, jangling her bracelets. "Close your eyes."

I sighed. I had Lightning Man comics to draw. "Donna, you're a nice lady, but you're not my type."

"Hush. Close your eyes."

I leaned back and reluctantly closed my eyes. "Now what?"

"Picture the man you were before your accident. Remember what his sex life was like."

Jesus. I never thought about this, but I remembered it so easily.

Before the accident, I was twenty-three, good-looking, athletic, rich, and smart. Witty. Friendly. I was every girl's dream, and I got dates whenever I wanted. Girlfriends. Any woman I set my eye on, I got.

I wasn't a player; I was one of those serial-relationship guys. Every few months I'd have a new girlfriend, each one more gorgeous and perfect than the last. And we'd have sex. Lots and lots of great, healthy, energetic sex—in every place, every position. The Andrew Mason before the accident had the best kind of sex there is, and tons of it.

Then I made one bad decision, and it all ended. That guy died, and the girlfriends disappeared. I wasn't the kind of guy any woman would look at anymore.

"Andrew?" Donna said.

"Yeah," I managed, my eyes still closed.

"Do you still see yourself as that man?"

The question was so absurd I laughed out loud, my eyes still closed. "You've got to be kidding me."

"You're still that man," Donna said. "He's still you. Sexually and otherwise."

I opened my eyes. I thought of Tessa Hartigan standing in front of my security camera, her blonde bob and her slim legs in shorts as she held up her cake. "Donna, this isn't going to work."

"If there's someone you're interested in, talk to her. Take chances. Take risks. Be that man." Donna smiled at me. "You never know what will happen."

"Except I do," I said. "I do know. I'll get turned down and pitied. And I'll feel worse than I did before. I can't go down that road again." The road I'd been on after the accident was the darkest place I'd ever been, and it had taken me years to recover. "It isn't somewhere I can go."

Donna looked at me for a long minute, her expression serious. She opened her mouth as if to say something. Then her expression cleared and she smiled again.

"Okay, then," she said. "I guess I'll try the herbs."

EIGHT

Tessa

IT WAS HOT. The worst heat wave in Michigan in ten years—the Internet said so—and the air conditioning in my grandmother's house was broken. I had found a small, 1980's-era oscillating fan in the basement, and I'd plugged it in next to the bed, but the whisper of air it gave off wasn't doing much to cool me off, even at nearly midnight.

Yet another night without sleep. I might become delirious.

I lay on top of my grandmother's bedspread, wearing only a tank top and a pair of panties, staring miserably at the ceiling and sweating. I had a busy day tomorrow: an interview at one of the bars I'd applied at and, incredibly, a modeling casting call. I'd found an ad for an open call for a catalog. I wasn't used to open calls anymore, but without an agent I had no choice but to try it. I needed to do what I did best: show up, wear underwear, and smile.

But without any sleep, I'd look terrible. I sighed and flopped over on the bed, trying to get closer to the fan.

Next to my pillow, my cell phone rang. It was Andrew Mason.

"Hello?" I said in surprise as I answered it.

"Your light is on," Andrew said. "Why is your light on?"

That voice. It instantly calmed my nerves and gave me that familiar shiver at the same time. "I can't sleep," I said.

"Why not?"

I rolled onto my back again. "It's hot," I panted.

He was quiet for so long I wondered if he'd hung up.

"Andrew?" I said.

He cleared his throat. "I'm here."

I realized what I'd said and how I'd said it. "Sorry. Did that sound sexual?"

"It's fine," Andrew said. "Totally fine. Is your air conditioning broken?"

"Yes. I called four different companies, but this is the worst heat wave in a decade and they're all booked solid. The earliest I could get someone to fix it is next week."

"That sucks. Do you have a fan?"

"Yes. It does nothing. I might not live until next week, in which case you'll be rid of me. Why are you awake so late?"

"I don't know," he said. "I can't sleep."

For the first time, I realized we weren't arguing, bantering, or —whatever it was we had done before. We were just talking, his voice low in my ear. I felt some of my nerves relax. "Are you in bed?" I asked him.

"Yeah. Where else would I be?"

"I don't know. It's a stupid question, I guess. I'm just curious about you. Your life."

"It isn't very interesting," Andrew said. "Ask me anything you want to know."

"Anything?"

"Sure."

"Okay. Are you in pain?"

He paused, as if the question was something he didn't usually think about. "Not really. Not like you think. The muscles in my back and my hips can get knotted. The injury itself doesn't hurt anymore."

"Anymore?"

"Not after the first two years."

Two years? He'd had two years of pain? "Okay. Are you in your wheelchair all the time?"

"When I want to get around, so usually yes. Otherwise I'm on my couch or in bed. Or in the shower."

"And your legs don't work at all? There's nothing the doctors can do?"

He surprised me again with his honesty. "I have sensation to mid-thigh, then nothing. My hips move but not my knees or my ankles. They can't do anything about it now, but by the time I'm old they'll probably be able to do amazing shit. Make a spine in a 3D printer or connect the nerves with nanobots or something. Some guy a hundred years from now is going to think I lived in the Dark Ages."

"That's an optimistic view."

"I'm the least optimistic guy you've ever seen."

I smiled at my ceiling. "I want to meet you. Can I come over?"

"You really don't, and no. It's the middle of the night."

"I'll be quiet."

"No. Now it's time for you to answer personal questions," Andrew said. "Why are you in Michigan and not L.A.?"

So I told him. I told him about my hippie parents, my grandmother, my life. I told him how I'd ended up in L.A. modeling, but when I inherited this house I'd packed my bags and left.

"Sounds like you didn't like it much," he said when I finished.

"I don't know," I replied honestly. "I left home at seventeen. I just needed to be gone. I was used to being on my own, anyway. L.A. and modelling seemed like it would be glamorous and fun. Instead I lived in dives and dated jerks and went on soul-crushing auditions. I didn't *tell* myself I didn't like it. Yet when I got the opportunity to leave, I did."

"Michigan, though," Andrew said. "Seriously. Michigan."

I laughed. "It isn't so bad. The neighbors are nice, when their kids aren't being little shits on Halloween."

"Yeah, about that. Can I confess something?"

"I might regret this, but yes."

He paused. "The Hi cake was fucking delicious."

I laughed again, louder this time. "I knew you liked my cake. I knew it!"

"Okay, fine," he said. "You've said hi. So hi."

I grinned to myself. I had that giddy feeling you get when you're talking to a gorgeous, smart, amazing single guy, and he's said *hi*. The best feeling, really.

He's in a wheelchair, Tessa.

It should matter. It really should. I should back off.

Instead, I said, "Hi, Andrew. Nice to meet you."

"You too. Now go to sleep."

I sighed. "You're right. I have an audition tomorrow and I need to look fresh."

"A bra audition? That's a thing?"

"Yes. So I need my beauty sleep."

"Turn your light out or I'll worry."

I reached over and switched off my lamp. "Better?"

"Better. Good night."

"Good night."

We hung up and I lay in the darkness, sweating. And I pictured Andrew Mason in bed.

I didn't mind that picture at all.

NINE

Andrew

TESSA DIDN'T GET her beauty sleep.

I didn't get much either, but I got a little. Enough for me. I was up early the next morning, drinking my coffee as the sun rose high and started baking the street outside. I turned on the monitor showing the house across the street just as Tessa came out her front door.

She had on a loose, flowing top, practically a piece of cotton. Peeking from the wide neck I could see the straps of a bikini tied at the back of her neck. She wore shorts and flip-flops, no makeup, her hair messy. She walked slowly out of her front door, opened her car, fished in the front seat for something. Then she walked back to her door.

She looked fucking exhausted. Even on the monitor I could see it, the way her walk didn't have any bounce to it. She ran a hand through her hair in a tired gesture and disappeared back into the house.

I picked up my phone. Hesitated.

This is a bad idea.

It was creepy, for one thing. It was weird enough that I'd called her last night when I'd seen her light on—I shouldn't even have been looking. Now I was looking again.

But that wasn't the only reason. It was just a bad idea. Very, very bad.

This isn't going to work out.

She isn't interested in you, even as a friend. No one is.

You're going to get hurt.

I held the phone in my hand and I closed my eyes.

Do it.

Don't do it.

Try something. Do it.

No. Don't.

Jesus, everything was so fucking hard.

Tessa had been friendly to me. Even when I was a dick to her, she'd been friendly. Maybe I could be friendly in return for once in my life. Just... nice. Like a normal person.

You're not a normal person.

"No, but I can pretend to be one," I said out loud, my voice a rasp in the quiet. Then I took a breath and dialed her number.

She answered, her voice flat. "Hey, Andrew."

"Did you get any sleep?" I asked her, as if I didn't know.

Tessa sighed. "No. The heat is so awful and they say it isn't going to break soon. It's hitting me today, you know? The air conditioner has been broken since I got here, and I haven't had a good night's sleep."

She'd moved in what, a week ago? No wonder she was so tired. "What time is your audition?" I asked her.

"Four. Then I have an interview for a bartending job at six."

I glanced at the clock. "It's only eight right now."

"I know. It's early, but I wasn't sleeping so I thought I might as well get up, and—"

"If you come here, you can get a few hours before you have to go to your audition."

There was silence on the other end of the line.

I closed my eyes. *Nice job, fuckface. Here it comes.*

Then Tessa's voice came over the line. "Really? You'd let me do that?"

She sounded like she was about to cry. "I think lack of sleep has made you emotional, but yes. My air conditioning works fine."

"You have a spare bedroom?"

"No. I have one bedroom, but since it's morning I'm not using it right now. I have light-blocking shades and it's cool. I don't have anyone coming today so it'll be quiet. I'll just be working at my computer. You could probably get six, seven hours. It makes no difference to me."

"Oh my God," she said. "Please, please don't change your mind. Give me ten minutes. I'll be right there."

"Tessa?"

She hung up.

TEN MINUTES later she appeared on my front door security camera, a bag over her shoulder. She was waving, tired but excited. I took another breath and pressed the code to let her in.

I heard the front door open and close, and her flip-flops coming down the short hall. Then she came into the living room. In the flesh. Wearing the bikini top, the loose shirt, the shorts. Her legs were slim and perfect. Her bobbed hair was a spiky, sweaty mess. She had no makeup on, and she'd left off the giant sunglasses. Her eyes were soft blue, her lashes dark. Her cheeks were flushed with heat and exhaustion. She was so fucking gorgeous I could hardly breathe.

We stared at each other in silence for a minute. I realized she was looking at me the same way I was looking at her—up and down, taking in every detail. Then she smiled—a real smile, one with actual happiness in it.

"Hi," she said.

"Hi," I replied.

Her gaze wandered the room. This used to be a living room once, but I'd transformed it. On one side was my sofa and chair, but on the other I'd put in my workstation, including a small bank of monitors, my drawing tablet and pen, and two keyboards. The whole thing looked high-tech, and her eyes widened a little. Then she looked back at me, sitting in my chair. I was wearing black sweatpants and a gray T-shirt and I hadn't shaved this morning, though I had showered. I had socks on my feet. I wondered what she saw when she looked at me.

She put her bag down. "I could kiss you," she said.

"No," I said.

She sighed. "Can I at least thank you?"

"In a non-physical way, I suppose." I gestured to myself. "I realize this is spectacular and hard to resist, but I ask that you try."

Her eyes widened. "It is spectacular," she said, and I couldn't tell if she was playing along with the joke or not. She lowered herself and sat on the sofa. "It's nice in here. I like it."

"It's a man cave, and you don't have to be sociable. You can just go to sleep if you want."

"It is sort of a man cave." She looked around and sniffed a little, as if she could smell testosterone. "I've spent the last week in my grandma's old-lady cave, though, so I find it refreshing."

"Fair enough. Does she have poufy curtains?"

"Yes, flowered. And a china cabinet with china she never used."

"I feel for you, then. Enjoy my tech gadgets and dirty socks."

I didn't have dirty socks, actually. I did my laundry, and I had cleaners who regularly cleaned my house. But still.

Tessa pointed at my workstation. "What do you do there?"

I ticked off on my fingers. "Code things. Draw comics. Hack websites when I'm bored. Monitor my security system. Watch porn."

She politely raised her eyebrows. "Oh, really? Sounds lovely."

"It is."

"I've always wanted to meet my dream man."

"Of course you have. I'll consider it, but you'll have to compete with the other women."

She looked around pointedly. "What other women?"

"If I told you, the competition wouldn't be fair, would it?"

She grinned at me. A goofy grin, like she was giddy. "Right."

I let her stare at me for another minute, punchy with exhaustion, and then I raised my eyebrows. "Well? Are you going to go sleep in my bedroom or not?"

Tessa closed her eyes. "I might just nap on this sofa, I'm so tired."

"Please don't." I couldn't watch her sleep, those long legs and that bikini top. "Go in the bedroom and close the door so I don't hear you snore."

"But I feel rude. I've barely even said hello."

"We've talked plenty, and I told you not to be sociable. I sure as hell am not." I paused, then said more sincerely, "Tessa, go sleep. We can talk when you wake up. The bedroom is down the hall."

She rubbed her face. "Okay." She stood up and left the room. I heard my bedroom door close softly behind her.

She was probably asleep in minutes. She had no idea I sat

there for a long while after she left, smelling the remains of her scent in the air. Thinking about her in my bed. And wondering what the hell I'd gotten myself into.

TEN

Tessa

ANDREW MASON MAY BE AN ASSHOLE, but his bed was heaven.

It was big, and cool, and perfectly soft. The sheets were dark gray, the manliest possible color except for black. As promised, there were blackout shades on the windows, which I gleefully used to block out the burning hot day outside. Then I tossed off my flip-flops and got in bed.

It smelled good. Clean. A little masculine, but not gross. I pictured Andrew getting in and out of this bed. How exactly did he do it? There were no handle bars on the walls. Nothing that indicated someone whose legs were paralyzed lived here.

Did he sleep naked?

Did he sleep alone?

A guy in a wheelchair could get dates, especially if he looked like *that*. Dark hair, trim dark beard, incredible cheekbones. Eyes that had a gleam of relentless intelligence and missed nothing.

Tightly muscled chest. Standing in front of him, in person for the first time, I'd felt like his gaze stripped me naked in the very best way.

His shoulders were hot, too, as were his arms in his T-shirt. I had a weakness for nice biceps.

For the first time, I let myself wonder if his injury had affected his ability to have sex.

I shouldn't be thinking about him like that—as if he were a piece of meat. He was my neighbor, and he had a life that was much harder than mine. He was doing me a favor. Aside from his looks—and his prickly personality—I actually liked him. He was funny and smart and fascinating. I was lonely here in Michigan. Okay, to be honest, I'd been lonely in L.A., too. All my life, really. It felt good that I'd found someone I could be friends with.

"Friends," I mumbled to myself, snuggling into the pillow that smelled like him. "Definitely friends." And then I tumbled into nothingness.

I WOKE TO COOL DARKNESS. I was groggy and completely relaxed. I hadn't slept so well since leaving L.A. Since before that, in fact—my last apartment in L.A. was hot and the walls were paper-thin.

I rolled over and blinked sleepily. Then I remembered my audition.

I bolted out of bed and opened the bedroom door, stepping out into the hallway, sweat breaking on my skin. Where the hell was I, and what time was it?

"Relax," said a familiar voice. "You're not late."

I turned. At the end of the short hallway was the living room, where Andrew was sitting at his work station. He was quietly bent over his graphics tablet, pen in hand, his features still with concentration. His profile was to me, and I stared at him for a second as I got my bearings.

Andrew paused what he was doing and turned his head, looking at me. His eyebrows went up. "You okay?"

"What time is it?" I asked, my voice a rasp.

"Two-thirty."

I blinked, doing the math. "I've been asleep for *six hours?*"

"I guess you were tired."

Jesus. It had felt like ten minutes, tops. I touched my hair, which I could feel was standing on end. My clothes were askew and I probably had red pillow-marks on my face. "Uh," I said, suddenly self-conscious. "I guess I'll clean up."

"Bathroom is to your right," Andrew said.

In the bathroom mirror, I was a disaster. I was sweaty and wild-eyed, a warmed-over cadaver. I patted my hair ineffectually, then remembered I was going to a casting call. In which I was supposed to look good.

There was a brief knock on the door. "You want your bag?" Andrew asked, as if reading my mind. "You can take a shower if you want."

I opened the door to find him just outside, holding my bag out to me. "You're being awfully nice to me," I said, taking it.

"The sooner you shower, the sooner you leave," he said logically. "Also, in return for my hospitality, you can make me a sandwich when you're done."

"I never agreed to that," I said.

"You will. I'm just thinking of a way to word it."

I closed the door in his face.

His bathroom was spacious—big enough to accommodate his wheelchair. The vanity was low, I realized, as was the mirror. The shower had a bench in it.

"When in Rome," I said to myself, and started stripping my clothes off.

ELEVEN

Tessa

"YOU KNOW WHAT?" I said half an hour later as I sat on Andrew's couch, eating a sandwich. "I liked sitting down in the shower. It's relaxing and civilized."

Andrew bit into his own sandwich—which, in the end, I'd made him. Turkey, mayo, and fancy mustard, just as he ordered. "I'm glad you find my shitty life interesting," he said.

I lowered my sandwich. "Am I being offensive?"

He paused, too. "Are you going to ask me every thirty seconds if you're being offensive?"

We stared at each other for a second. "Okay," I said, "let's make a deal. If I'm being offensive, just tell me off."

"I do that anyway," Andrew said.

"Yes, but that might just be because of your everyday crabbiness. The point is, I don't actually know when I'm being offensive."

Andrew shrugged and put the last of his sandwich into his

mouth. "Do you want a code word or something?" he asked. "If I say it, you'll know you're being an ass."

I blinked. "You mean like a safe word?"

"Something like that. How about this? If you're being offensive, I'll say 'Bea Arthur.' Then you'll know."

"Bea Arthur? Are you for real?"

"It's as good a safe word as any."

I laughed. "I'm not sure why I like you."

"Me neither. Probably because I have air conditioning. How do you become a bra model, anyway?"

I swallowed my bite of sandwich and took a drink of water. I was showered and dressed in a navy blue sundress, and I felt like a new woman. A new, hungry woman. "Well, you start by traveling the country with your hippie parents, who don't supervise you as much as they should. Then you develop boobs and catch the eye of sketchy older men who say they want to take pictures of you."

Andrew froze mid-bite. "Are you fucking serious?"

"Yes, I am." I shrugged. "I was never actually assaulted, but I chalk that up to pure luck and survival instinct. I'd been in some dangerous situations by the time I was fourteen." Those experiences had led me to crash and burn, but I didn't want to talk about that. "Anyway, looking pretty was what I knew how to do, so when I was sixteen I signed up with a reputable modeling agency and tried to get work. That was in Denver. My first gig was modeling a nursing bra, if you can believe it." I put down my drink and mimed. "I had to pose demonstrating the clasp, you know? The one here that opens the nipple flap. I was seventeen. I made a hundred and fifty dollars."

Andrew leaned back in his chair. "That is deeply weird. And not a little disturbing."

"There's a whole world of modeling out there," I said. "Not everyone goes on a runway, wearing Victoria's Secret. Bras have been sold in catalogs for decades, and *someone* has to model them. Hand modeling is a big thing, too, though my hands aren't quite nice enough. There's watch modeling. I knew one woman in L.A. whose specialty was shampoo and hair spray ads. She stood with her back to the camera and did this." I shook my hair, brushing it back from my shoulders, though of course my hair was too short to demonstrate properly. "Before I cut my hair I did some calls, but my hair wasn't quite right. I also did some leg auditions—for razor and legging ads. Legs are hard, though. They have to be perfect, and you can't fake it. My calves are too thin."

Andrew was watching me, his sandwich in his hand. "Your legs are nice," he said.

That gave me that giddy feeling again, the one you get when a great-looking guy notices that your legs are nice. "Thanks," I said. "Nice doesn't cut it in the modeling world, though."

"Huh," he said thoughtfully. He took a bite of sandwich and swallowed. "It sounds like your whole career is about being told your body parts are subpar."

"It sounds that way, but I'm used to it. It's better than being a nurse, I guess. Less schooling, and not as much work."

"You wanted to be a nurse?"

Of all the topics we'd talked about, that one made my cheeks burn. I didn't know why I'd said that; I never talked about wanting to be a nurse with anyone. "I know, it sounds dumb. A bra model wanting to be a nurse. I don't have the brains, and I definitely don't have the money."

Andrew frowned, thinking. "You would if you sold your grandmother's house."

"But then I'd have nowhere to live."

He was watching me closely with that gaze that missed nothing. "Still, you've thought about it," he said like a psychic. "It's one of the reasons you left L.A."

No. There was no way that Tessa Hartigan, daughter of

hippies and semi-failed model, was going to be a nurse. So I did what I always did when I wanted to distract a man: I changed the topic to sex.

"I left L.A. because, as you say, none of my body parts were quite good enough. Except for these." I straightened my spine and gestured at my boobs, now demurely covered by the navy blue dress. "These, I'll have you know, are flawless. Every casting director says so. In fact, you might be looking at the world's most perfect breasts, right here."

He narrowed his eyes as if he saw through my ruse, and then he corrected me. "I'm not looking at them."

It was true. His eyes were carefully aimed at my face. I suddenly wished he would look lower, which was the opposite of how I felt with every other man. I wanted Andrew to see. "Do you know what makes the world's most perfect breasts?" I asked him, pushing him harder.

"Tessa, really."

That shiver again when he said my name. I loved this—getting a reaction from him, seeing if I could make it the reaction I wanted. "It isn't just size," I explained. "The shape matters. Like a teardrop. They can't sit too high or hang too low. Fake boobs don't work for the really good casting agents—the boobs don't look quite right, and sometimes they're uneven or the scars show. Mine are real, of course."

It was working. He was definitely distracted now. "Of course," he said.

"They also have to be proportioned correctly with my torso." I gestured to the sides of my ribcage. "It has to be pleasing to the eye. It's mathematical. My body is x wide, so my breasts are—"

"Okay." Andrew's voice sounded a little choked. "I get the idea."

"Oh, please. I thought you watched porn all day. You don't want to talk about breasts?"

He ran a hand through his hair. "It isn't my usual topic of conversation, no. But please continue."

I watched his expression. Was he turned on? Why did I hope the answer was yes? I spent most of my time fighting men off. Why did I want Andrew to get closer?

And still, I hadn't pushed far enough. I could never leave well enough alone. "Do you want to see them?" I asked him. I put a hand to the strap of my dress, as if to pull it down.

Andrew put his sandwich plate down next to him. "No, Tessa, I do not."

I tugged the strap half an inch. "They're really impressive. I have a bra on."

"I'm sure they are, but no. Keep your dress on, please."

I dropped my hand and sighed in disappointment. "You're the first man who's ever said that to me."

Andrew was silent. For a second his gaze was dark and intense, looking at my face, my throat, and yes, my breasts through the navy blue dress.

I was playing with fire. And I liked it. My blood was hot in my veins, my ears buzzing. I had the urge to touch him. A hand on his arm, anything. I bet he would be warm, his skin firm. I had always liked the way men felt, the way they smelled. I'd just always ended up touching the wrong men.

"Is that what you do at these casting calls?" Andrew asked, his voice low and serious. "Just show up and take off your shirt?"

"That's the idea."

"You don't even know these guys."

He was concerned, I realized. It only made me want to touch him more. "It's professional," I told him. "I realize it doesn't sound like it, but this is business. There are other models there, plus photographers, marketing people, assistants. It isn't a creepy audition in a back room."

"Still, text me when you get there," he said. "And while you're there. And when you're leaving."

I swallowed, touched. Everyone in L.A. was so hungry, so busy striving for the same selfish version of success, that they never looked out for each other. I wasn't used to it. I could handle myself; I'd handled myself at dozens of auditions. And still, I said, "Okay, I will."

"And you know what? Text me from the bartending interview, too. Guys who run bars can be fucking creeps, even if you keep your dress on."

"Okay," I said again. "I'll be careful, Andrew. I always am."

He was quiet for another moment. Then he looked away as if something had hurt him, his face hard.

"Good," he said. "Now finish your sandwich and get going. You don't want to be late."

TWELVE

Tessa: I'm here at the casting call. In the waiting room. There are other models here. We're hanging out, waiting for our turn.

Andrew: Good. Also, that director has a hard job.

Tessa: You'd be amazed how many of them are gay. Makes things simpler sometimes.

Andrew: Do you still have clothes on?

Tessa: For the moment, yes. What are you doing?

Andrew: Right now? Sending Lightning Man on a mission to the underworld, where someone is posing as his evil twin. The evil twin has fooled Judy Gravity and Lightning Man must rescue Judy and save her life.

Tessa: ...

Andrew: What?

Tessa: I think that might be the best answer I've ever read in my life.

Andrew: It's just comics. It isn't literal rocket science.

Tessa: Still, oh my god. Your life is very cool.

Andrew: Hello? Wheelchair.

Tessa: You're still cool, sorry.

Andrew: You need a wider circle of friends.

Tessa: So we're friends now?

Andrew: I admit nothing.

Tessa: They're calling me, I gotta go.

TESSA: Okay, I'm changed and in the dressing room now. To prove I'm okay, here's a selfie.

Andrew: I did not need a photo of you in your underwear.

Tessa: Technically not MY underwear, but you're still lying. You liked it.

Andrew: I've deleted it.

Tessa: Okay, here's another one.

Andrew: ...

Tessa: You're typing and not sending anything.

Andrew: ...

Tessa: Still doing it.

Andrew: I'm terrified I'll get another photo if I send anything.

Tessa: Send me one back.

Andrew: I'm dressed. And I don't do selfies. Literally ever.

Tessa: Take your shirt off and do it, Mason. Expand your horizons, I dare you.

Andrew: If you're trying to get me naked, it won't work. I recognize the signs. Women try to get me naked all the time.

Tessa: They're calling me again, gotta go.

TESSA: Can I ask you something?

Andrew: Does this mean the casting call is over?

Tessa: Yes. I'm dressed and everything. I still have a question.

Andrew: Okay.

Tessa: I was bored, and I was Googling things. My question is kind of personal. Okay, it's very personal.

Andrew: Oh, God, here it comes.

Tessa: What?

Andrew: You're going to ask about sex.

Tessa: Wait, what? People ask you about that?

Andrew: It's the number one thing people are curious about. You see why I don't leave the house.

Tessa: What is wrong with people? That is so fucking rude.

Andrew: Are you going to try and tell me that wasn't your question?

Tessa: No, it totally was my question. But we're friends. I gave you a Hi cake. I slept in your bed. You've seen me in my underwear!

Andrew: Fine. I'll fill you in. Some people with spinal injuries have it worse than I do. My legs and feet don't work, but I can take a shit by myself, I can do anything that doesn't involve walking, and I can fuck. Does that satisfy your curiosity?

Tessa: A little excessively, but yes. So you have girlfriends?

Andrew: Sure, women flock to me. Seriously, Tessa, what do you think?

Tessa: I think you need work. Luckily you have me to take you on.

Andrew: Don't you have an interview to go to?

THIRTEEN

Andrew

IT DIDN'T SEEM POSSIBLE, but for the next few days Tessa and I settled into a sort of routine. During the day, I did my thing while she ran errands or tried to get auditions. She got the bartending job, so she'd go to the bar from four until midnight. When she was done her shift, she'd come back to my house to mooch my air conditioning and sleep in my bed.

Without me, of course. I slept on the sofa.

We'd argued about it long and hard. I wanted to be a gentleman and give her the bed. Tessa didn't want to make a guy in a wheelchair sleep on the sofa. Both of us felt like an asshole, and neither of us wanted to give in. But I pulled rank in the end because it was my house, so I gave her the bed and took the couch.

It didn't matter much to me. My sofa was actually pretty comfortable. That wasn't what was pissing me off.

What was pissing me off was that I'd been stupid. I'd broken my own rule. I'd let Tessa in. And now I wanted her there.

I liked her there all the time, no matter what she was doing. Even when she was invading my bathroom or drinking the soda in my fridge. Sometimes she hung out with me quietly while I drew, reading back issues of Lightning Man comics and eating my snacks. Sometimes she talked, which in turn made me talk.

I never talked. Not if I could help it. But with Tessa, I talked.

"I don't know," Tessa said a few days later as she came out of the kitchen. I was sitting on the sofa, surfing the internet on my laptop. She handed me a glass of ice water and sat down next to me. "I think the best Spider-Man was the first one. Or was it the second one? The one where he kisses her while he's hanging upside down."

I rolled my eyes. "The usual layman's opinion."

She sipped her iced tea. She was wearing a knee-length skirt of some kind of thin, swishy material and a tank top. "There's such a thing as an expert in Spider-Man?"

"Is there such a thing as an expert in bra modeling?"

Her blue eyes widened. "Touché."

"That version of Spider-Man isn't the best one," I said. "Everyone knows that."

"What's the best version?"

"They haven't made it yet."

"So they have to keep making them over and over forever?"

I raised my eyebrows. "Is there a question in there?"

She leaned back against the cushions, smiling. "Right. Comic-book geek."

"What tipped you off? The fact that I've illustrated hundreds of pages of comics, maybe?"

She sipped her iced tea. "Your comics are better than any of the Spider-Man movies," she said dutifully.

I clicked another page on the website I was on. "I told you, I don't write them. Nick does. Do you like pickles?"

"Excuse me?"

"I'm ordering groceries. I know you like terrible bright-yellow mustard on your sandwiches, but I don't know if you like pickles."

She folded one long, bare leg and tucked her foot under her other thigh. Whoever said her calves were too skinny was either blind or crazy. "I love pickles. You don't?"

"Sure, I love something that reeks of salty, disgusting brine. What's not to like?" I clicked the pickles and added them to my cart.

"But you're still ordering them," she said.

"Because I'm an excellent host, yes. I'm also ordering the yellow mustard." I also added ginger ale, because she liked that, too.

"My sandwiches are going to be amazing," Tessa said, smiling. "Maybe I won't get my air conditioning fixed after all."

She had a repairman scheduled to come in two days. Then she'd go back to her house, because she'd have no reason to come to mine. It crossed my mind to go across the street and sabotage her fucking air conditioning just to keep her here, but I wasn't very agile and I'd probably get caught. So I tried not to think about being alone again.

Nick was due back in a few days, anyway. But the words of Donna the wellness therapist came back into my head. *He's found his union with another. That leaves you alone. The honeymoon only outlines what you know deep down is true.*

Nick was married now. Maybe there'd even be a kid soon, or more than one. Sad old Uncle Andrew in the wheelchair was going to get fewer and fewer visits.

Yeah, maybe I'd still sabotage Tessa's air conditioning. Her heat, too, so she'd have to stay here in winter.

"What's Nick like?" Tessa asked, as if she was reading the thoughts going through my mind. "You don't have any family photos in this house or anything."

"Nick is ugly," I said emphatically, clicking to check out my grocery cart. "He's hideous. His personality sucks. It's possible he's a serial killer. He has zero personal hygiene. And he is very, very married."

She licked a drop of iced tea off her bottom lip, and every nerve below my waist jangled. The ones that still worked, anyway. "So he's hot and awesome like you," she said. "Interesting. I'd like to meet him."

"You're forgetting about the married part," I reminded her. "Also, he's gay. Married *and* gay. Not someone who would interest you at all."

"He's that great, huh?" She gave me a look that made my working nerves jangle again. She was only a few feet away from me on the sofa, and I could smell her scent. It was the same scent that was on my sheets and pillows at the moment. "Are you jealous of your brother, Andrew?"

I wasn't. That was the truth. Even when I was whole, I'd never felt like I was in competition with Nick. I'd been too successful on my own, and besides, I was the older brother. It was Nick who looked up to me.

After the accident, our entire relationship had changed so completely that I wasn't sure I'd ever understand it. Nick was my blood and my lifeline. He'd seen me through literally the darkest moments of my life, the moments when I didn't want to live anymore. He was also the one who was still whole, the one who could go live the life I couldn't. Jealousy was too simple a word for what I felt for my brother.

Still, looking at Tessa, I had never been so glad in my life that Nick was married. If he was single, she probably wouldn't look at me.

"I will admit," I said to Tessa, "that my brother is slightly good-looking. Not as good-looking as me, of course."

"It isn't possible for any guy to be as good-looking as you," Tessa said, and once again I didn't know if she was playing along with the joke or not.

"I'm glad you noticed," I said, deciding to assume she was joking. "What happened with the casting call, by the way?"

She pulled out her phone and looked at it, scrolling through her messages. "I haven't heard from them yet."

"Does that mean no, or that they haven't decided who to hire yet?"

"It could mean either one." She shrugged. "Welcome to the modeling business. Ninety-nine percent of your time is spent in uncertainty. That's the job."

"They'd be crazy not to hire your boobs," I said, since she'd complimented my comics. "I'm sure they were the best boobs there."

"Thank you, Andrew. That's very sweet." She smiled at me.

A minute ago I'd been hot and awesome, and now I was sweet. How far into the friend zone was I? I had no idea, and it wasn't even her fault. I kept myself in the friend zone, even though my working nerves really didn't want to be there. I was truly fucked up.

She was so close. What would she do if I reached out and touched her?

I thought about it, and then I thought about what her face would look like when she rejected me. Sad and pitying? Or offended and angry?

So I didn't do it.

We were friends. That was all.

FOURTEEN

Tessa

THE BAR I'd gotten a job at was called Miller's. It was in a strip mall next to a cluster of big-box stores, near a gym and, yes, the Cheesecake Factory. It seemed like a decent enough place—more of a family-friendly pub than a dive. There was brunch on Sundays and local musical acts—probably terrible—on Saturday nights. I got four shifts a week behind the bar to start, with the possibility for five. I wore jeans and a black T-shirt with the Miller's logo on the breast. Tonight I was wiping the bar after pouring four beers and making a gin and tonic for the few customers that came to Miller's at seven o'clock on a Thursday night.

I checked that the owner, Nathan, wasn't in sight anywhere, and then I pulled my phone from my back pocket. I texted Andrew.

Tessa: I have a question.

Andrew: Here we go.

Tessa: Does anyone ever call you Andy?

There was a brief pause, and then he replied.

Andrew: Andy? Did you just ask me that?

Tessa: So the answer is no, then.

Andrew: The answer is unquestionably, unequivocally, unapologetically, absolutely fucking no.

The big words again. I loved it when he used the big words. I wished I had him on the phone, so he could say them in my ear. But I couldn't exactly call him and ask him to talk dirty to me, so instead I texted him again.

Tessa: Point taken. I have another question.

Andrew: You always do.

Tessa: My boss kinda, sorta came on to me at the bar tonight. What should I do?

There was a long pause. The longest. My heart squeezed, then tried to climb up my throat in suspense.

I didn't know what I wanted him to say. Did I want him to be mad? Possessive? We weren't dating or anything—we were friends. Did I want him to encourage me? I had no idea. I didn't know what he felt, what he'd want to say. So I waited.

Finally the dots appeared, and he answered me.

Andrew: It depends if he's your type or not. Is he?

Tessa: Not really. He isn't a bad guy, and it wasn't creepy or anything. He's over thirty and I think he's divorced. It seemed like he was working up to asking me out, if you know what I mean, and not a Me Too-type thing. Does that make sense?

Andrew: You're saying he's single and he honestly finds you attractive.

Tessa: Yes.

My stomach was in knots, and I didn't know why. It wasn't because of Nathan. Nathan was okay, I guessed. He was male and he was interested in me. I wasn't a girl who slept around, but I liked it when a man was interested in me. I liked men in general. Ever since I grew boobs, I could get men to at least look at me, and it made me feel good. It was just the way I was made.

If I was back in L.A., I'd at least give Nathan a chance. Go on a date and see what happened.

And now, I was texting Andrew, undecided. What did that mean?

"Tessa?"

I looked up to see Nathan coming out from the back room, smiling at me. Shit. Four days on the job, and I'd been caught texting. "Sorry," I said, putting my phone in my back pocket.

"It's fine," Nathan said, coming around behind the bar. "I had to give in a long time ago. There's no way I can make an employee work a full shift without looking at their phone." He shrugged. "I can't stay off it myself, so I may as well not be an asshole about it."

See? Nice. He was nice. He had brown hair worn longish and a pleasant face. He wasn't fat. He wore a button-down shirt that was pressed. Since he was single, he must have pressed the shirt himself. That was a point in his favor, too.

And I couldn't help the feeling that if I went on a date with him, it would be a disappointment. That I would rather be with Andrew.

Nathan looked around, checking that there were no customers who needed my attention. "Listen, Tessa, I'd like to talk to you about something. And please don't take it the wrong way."

So he was going to ask now. Okay then. "Sure, Nathan," I said.

He smiled. "Call me Nate."

His lips moved as he said something else, probably asking me out. But for a second I didn't hear him, because he'd asked me to call him Nate. Just like I'd asked Andrew about being called Andy.

His words went through my head, and I realized I agreed with them.

The answer is unquestionably, unequivocally, unapologetically, absolutely fucking no.

I heard Nathan—Nate—out. I was polite about it. And then I turned him down. I didn't want to be mean, and I appreciated the offer, so I told him I was "sort of seeing someone." I didn't tell him that the guy was my friend, and I'd just asked him whether I should take the date or not.

Then someone ordered drinks. And someone else. An hour later, when I looked at my phone, I saw that Andrew hadn't answered my question. He hadn't texted anything at all.

FIFTEEN

Andrew

I USUALLY DID thirty pull-ups in a session. Today I did sixty.

My arms were burning. So were my shoulders, my spine, and my abs. Pull-ups are easier when you keep tension in your legs and core. But my legs were dead weight from the knees down, so every pull-up was harder for me than it would be for someone whose legs worked.

Sweat rolled down my back, my chest. I kept my abs flexed as I pulled, hauling my body up for rep after rep. My hair was soaked. I thought I might throw up.

My front doorbell rang.

I lowered myself off the bar onto the bench beneath it and picked up my phone. Looked at the security monitor. If it was Tessa, this time I was going to ignore her. I was too fucked up right now, too tangled to be near her.

Since her last text to me last night, we hadn't talked. And

after her shift was over, she hadn't come here to sleep. She'd gone home instead.

I'd monitored the security feed for her, so I knew she'd come home just after midnight last night and hadn't left her house since. Yes, I was fucking pathetic, but even if she wasn't coming here I wanted to make sure she got home safe. I couldn't sleep if I didn't know.

Even when she was killing me, I had to know she was okay.

It wasn't Tessa at the front door. It was my mother.

I sighed. My mother didn't visit regularly. Even though she'd made a sincere effort to get back into my life over the past few years, she still visited at random times, as if she came over whenever she remembered I existed. Donna the wellness therapist said that I had to "put healing energy" into the relationship with my mother. My real therapist, the one with actual qualifications, said I had to "set boundaries." It was a toss-up to me as to which one of them was more full of shit.

Still, I let Mom in. "I'm back here," I called to her when I heard the front door close.

Mom came back to the spare bedroom I'd turned into a workout room, with weights and lift bars fitted so they were easy for me to use. She was wearing linen pants and a sleeveless silk blouse, her hair— dark like mine, but streaked with gray—tied up neatly in a bun. My mother was in her mid-fifties, rich, a great dresser, and newly single. Frankly, she was a bit of a babe. It was only a matter of time before some rich, handsome guy snapped her up and married her.

Then there'd be another wedding, another honeymoon. Another person moving on with their life without me.

"Hi," she said, coming into the room as I mopped sweat from my face and neck with a towel. She kissed me on the cheek and handed me a gift bag. "I brought you something."

"Really, Mom," I said, but I took the bag. Since coming back into my life, my mother seemed to feel that she needed to bring me things—a book, a knick-knack, new underwear. She was also paying for Donna's therapy visits. It was like part of her had the impulse to buy her way back into my good graces. But the thought was sincere, and she really was trying, so I didn't have the heart to tell her to knock it off.

"You're really sweating," she said, lightly touching my hair as I opened the bag. "Are you overdoing it?"

"I'm fine," I said, though I could feel shaking in the muscles of my arms and back. Thinking about Tessa saying yes to her boss's offer of a date had made me wish I drank so I could black out my thoughts. Instead I worked out until I nearly fainted.

She was going to go on a date with a guy. A normal, nice guy with legs. She was going to go on a date with him, and eventually she was going to sleep with him. Because that was what normal, beautiful, single women did in the real world.

What did you think would happen, idiot? You should never have invited her over in the first place.

I pushed the thought away and opened the gift bag. It was a set of DVDs—all of the Star Trek movies. "What's this?" I said.

"You like sci-fi, right?" Mom said.

I did like sci-fi, in fact. I could watch any of these movies online anytime I wanted, but I didn't say that. She was trying so hard. So I said, "Thanks, Mom."

"You're welcome." She smiled at me. "Do you want something to eat?"

I'd worked out so hard that my stomach couldn't handle food right now. "No, I'm fine."

She looked me over, standing in front of where I sat, a frown on her brow. "Are you sure? You look thinner than last time I saw you. Have you lost weight?"

"No."

"Really? What do the doctors say? You shouldn't be losing weight, Andrew."

"I'm not losing weight."

"I just—"

I reached out and put my hand over hers, closed my fingers gently over hers. "Mom, a glass of water would be great. I'll change my shirt and come out in a minute. Okay?"

She looked in my eyes, and her expression relaxed a little. "Okay."

I KNEW why my mother worried. The last time she saw me before she left my life the last time, I hadn't seen her. I'd been unconscious in the hospital after I'd tried to kill myself by taking too many sleeping pills. It was my second attempt.

According to Nick, our mother had come to the hospital and looked at me for only a moment. Then she'd turned to Nick and told him it was too hard. That all of it was too hard. And then she'd walked out of the hospital and, except for generous transfers of money into our bank accounts, she hadn't talked to either of us again.

Years later, Mom went into therapy—hence the acquaintance with Donna—and split up with our father. Dad was still incommunicado, but Mom decided to try and make amends. It was harder for Nick to forgive her, because Nick was the one who had watched her turn her back and walk out the hospital door. He'd been the one who'd watched her decide to leave the two of us to deal with everything on our own.

Me? It was different for me. In a way, I understood why Mom walked out that day. I understood how I hurt her by doing what I did. I'd given up, and I'd tried to check out—twice. I'd thought I didn't matter, that no one would care, that everyone would be better off without the burden of me. I'd tried to bail. I couldn't exactly fault her for doing the same thing.

And it *was* hard. All of it. Yet somehow, I was still here.

When Mom came back, trying to make things right again, I forgave her. We still had shit to work out, and it would never be the same as it had been before my accident, but when you don't have many people, like me, you make every person count. It wasn't her fault that I'd done what I'd done, twice. It wasn't anyone's fault. Except maybe mine.

So when she visited, I let her in. I accepted her gifts. I let her get me a glass of water.

And when she left my life again, which she probably would, I could at least say I'd done that much.

I didn't keep any sleeping pills in the house. No Percocet or fentanyl, either. Not even alcohol.

And if I hated the dark, I tried to remember that the sun always came up again.

WE TALKED in the living room. At first Mom sat next to me, touching my arm or holding my hand. Then she got up and fussed, checking that there was nothing wrong in the house, that the schedule on the fridge was right, that the housekeepers were doing a good job, that I didn't need my laundry done. She talked to me about her life, her penthouse condo in downtown Mill-wood, her club, the charity boards she worked on. She talked about Nick and Evie—she liked Evie, though the relationship had taken a bit of time to warm up on both sides. Evie was suspicious of anyone who had hurt Nick as badly as my mother had.

"They come back tomorrow," Mom said. "The flight is a long one, but I think it gets in—Who is that?"

She was looking out my front window. I pulled up my security app, my stomach sinking. I had a good guess who she was talking about.

On the camera, I saw Tessa leaving her house and crossing the street, heading for my door.

"That's my new neighbor," I said. "Her name is Tessa." What the hell did she want? I didn't want her here.

"You're friends with the neighbor? How nice," Mom said. Then she looked closer. "Oh, my goodness. What does her shirt say?"

I could guess. It was probably the shirt she'd worn on the first day she moved in, which said *Get the fuck out of my business*. "Um, she's a bit eccentric," I said. Dread was settling in my stomach. "I didn't know she was coming over."

"What is she coming here for?"

"I don't know, but—"

"It would be rude not to say hello if she's your friend. Oh, and now she's seen me through the window. I'll go let her in."

"Wait, Mom—"

But she was already out of the room.

SIXTEEN

Tessa

I ADMIT IT: I'd chickened out.

I worked the rest of my shift last night without texting Andrew. Without calling him. I stayed in my overheated house last night, and I didn't text him this morning, either.

I went over and over it in my head. I should tell him that I'd said no to Nate. But then again, that sounded like I owed him that information, like we were in a relationship. Which we weren't.

He'd never answered me, so I didn't know if he cared if I said yes or not. Maybe he didn't. Did I want him to care?

Why was I overthinking this? We were friends, right? Friends shared things that happened to them. I'd had friends before, even male friends. Why was it so hard to be friends with Andrew Mason?

I was too confused to go to his house after my shift, to sleep in his bed as if we hadn't had that awkward conversation. Being in his house at night, alone with him, felt too intimate.

And here was the truth: I wasn't intimate with people. Friendly, yes. Sociable, even flirty—yes. But my parents had treated me more like a friend than as their child, and I'd been on my own early in life. I'd never had a best friend or a long-term boyfriend. Relationships like that didn't happen when you were trying to make it in L.A., where all relationships were shallow and a little bit selfish.

Even when I dated guys in L.A., there was a question of what that guy could do for me—or what I could do for him. If one of us had ever actually seen real success, the other would have been gone in a heartbeat. The relationships I had were never the kind that could withstand any sort of test. And, I realized, I had kept it that way on purpose.

It was easier. You didn't get hurt if it didn't really matter.

But now, I realized the truth: Andrew mattered. Whether he was my friend or something else, he mattered. And by not texting him, by not talking to him, I'd been an asshole. No friend would act the way I had.

So—after a long, sweaty night in which I tried vainly to sleep in my grandmother's bedroom, next to a fan—I got up my courage and decided to try and fix it. The phone wasn't going to cut it, either. I needed to go over there.

I put on my *Get the fuck out of my business* shirt, because that shirt always gave me courage. I put on jeans and flip-flops. And I walked over to Andrew's house.

I did not expect to see the woman in the front window.

Too late, I realized there was a car in Andrew's driveway. He had a guest, and she was watching me with a surprised look on her face. She said something, probably to Andrew, and then she vanished from the window. The front door opened as I stepped up onto the porch, my steps reluctant now.

The woman who stood in the doorway was in her mid-fifties, strikingly beautiful, and obviously Andrew's mother. The resemblance couldn't have been more clear. She smiled at me politely, and I knew how Andrew had been so blessed in the genetics department.

"Hi there," she said. "You must be Andrew's neighbor."

"I'm Tessa," I said, shaking her hand. I was sweating hard under my T-shirt, both from the heat and from nerves. "I live across the street."

"I'm Rita, Andrew's mother." The woman's gaze dropped briefly to my chest, then back up again. "How nice of you to visit. Come in."

Shit. Shit, shit, shit. I'd just met Andrew's mother while wearing a T-shirt that said *Get the fuck out of my business* on it. Way to go, Tessa. I followed her into the living room, where Andrew was sitting in his wheelchair. He was wearing nylon workout pants and a gray T-shirt that fitted his torso and showed off his chest and his tightly muscled arms. His dark hair was a bit mussed and he had that trim dark beard on his jaw, as if he hadn't shaved in a few days. His eyes when he looked at me were dark and tired and filled with some kind of pain I couldn't quite read. I felt my heart squeeze hard in my chest.

"Hey," I said.

He was fighting it. Whatever it was, the mood that was dragging him down, he was fighting it. I watched his face go hard and his gaze go intentionally cold, the walls going up. "You met my mother, I see," he said.

There was none of his usual humor, the back-and-forth, the teasing. Had I done this to him? Or had she?

"Would you like something to drink?" Rita asked. "There's juice in the fridge. And ginger ale, though I didn't think Andrew liked ginger ale."

I looked at him. He didn't like ginger ale. I did. "I'm fine, thanks," I said.

"Have a seat," Rita said.

I dropped onto the sofa. I probably shouldn't ignore Rita—she seemed like a perfectly nice woman—but I couldn't help it. The only person I wanted to look at was Andrew. "Can we talk?" I asked him.

"Not really," he said.

"I got a call this morning," I said. "From the casting agency. They say I got the job."

His expression got even harder, if that was possible, his jaw twitching. "That's great."

It was. It was great. I was going to model bras for a catalog and make a few thousand dollars just to stand there with my breasts barely covered. It was the thing I did, the thing I was good at. It was easy, much-needed money. "They want me to start tomorrow."

His voice was flat. "That's great, Tessa. Is that it?"

"Should I leave?" Rita asked.

"I have to be on set for nine o'clock tomorrow," I said to Andrew. "It's my day off from the bar, so that works out. The problem is that the air conditioner repairman comes tomorrow, and when I booked the appointment, I thought I would be home."

His face held no flicker of expression. "So you need someone to take care of it while you're out? That's fine. Tell them to come here when they arrive. I'll handle it."

I searched his face, trying to read what he was thinking. "That's really nice of you."

He shrugged.

The air was thick as molasses, and after a moment of silence Rita said, "You know, I don't really follow what's going on."

Andrew's gaze flicked past me to his mother. "It's okay, Mom. Tessa and I are friends."

That word, *friends*. The flat way he said it. The look in his eyes.

No. Fuck no. Fuck, fuck, *fuck* no.

I swallowed past the lump in my throat and turned toward Rita, addressing her myself. "The fact is, I was a complete asshole to Andrew yesterday, and I came over here to apologize."

Rita's lovely face went a little bit hard, and she crossed her arms over her chest. Something flickered behind her eyes that was deep and complicated, love and fear at once, and I wondered what she was thinking about. "I beg your pardon," she said in a voice that could probably terrify an army of wait staff. "Andrew doesn't need to be mistreated by anyone. Perhaps you should leave."

"Jesus, Mom." Andrew closed his eyes and pressed his fingertips tiredly to his forehead. "I'm not a toddler."

"Andrew, you know you—"

"Stop." He said it so sharply, with so much command, that I wondered what she'd been about to say. There was something beneath the words that I didn't understand. He opened his eyes and looked at Rita. "Mom, you can go now. I can talk to Tessa alone."

Behind my shoulder, I felt her hesitate. "I don't like this," she said. "I don't like that this strange woman admits that she's...that she's..."

"An asshole," I finished for her. "I think the T-shirt gives it away."

"Can't you go be *an asshole* to somebody else?" Rita said, obviously forcing the curse word out.

"Mom," Andrew said. "I can handle it. You can go."

She paused again, looking at him. Then she turned and left.

I didn't blame her for her attitude. I liked her for it, actually. At least someone, somewhere, was looking out for Andrew. Trying to protect him from people like me.

When the door closed behind her, I turned back to him. "We need to talk," I said.

"I'm not doing this."

I blinked at him. "What?"

"This." His eyes blazed now, and he motioned to the air between him and me. "Whatever this is. This thing. It's why I don't let anyone into my house, Tessa. Because *I don't do this.*"

"Do what?" I shot back. "Emotions? Friendship? Giving a shit about someone?"

"All of it."

"Well, it's too late. You're already doing it. I'm already here. And I was a jerk last night, and I'm fucking sorry."

"For what?" He was getting angry now, letting it show now that Rita was gone. "For getting asked out? For going on a date? For being a normal person who would like to meet someone and get laid? You're single, Tessa, and you're a fucking hot bra model. Go do what you need to do. It's none of my business."

"That isn't what I'm apologizing for," I said. "I'm apologizing for texting you about it like you're in the friend zone, when you're not."

That stopped him for a second, and then he was angry again. "Tessa, get real. I'm in the permanent friend zone. We both know it."

"Why?" I said. I pointed to his chair. "Because of that?"

"Not because of the fucking chair," Andrew said. "Because of the man who's in it."

Our gazes met for a long, silent second. Both of us were blazing hot, and my throat was still choked up. I stood up and walked toward him.

"Tessa," he said, his voice a low warning.

I ignored it. I stood in front of him and put my hands on the back of his chair, leaning over him. All the way down. Sure, I was wearing the obscene T-shirt, but underneath it I had nice tits and I wasn't afraid to use them. I never had been.

I bent lower, lower. Brushed my cheek against the stubble of his beard and felt it against my skin. I loved the feel of a man's beard, to be honest. Somehow harsh and soft at the same time.

He smelled good. I knew he would, because I'd smelled his scent in the bed I'd slept in. Clean, soapy, a little bit sweaty because he'd probably been working out. I nuzzled him lightly, feeling the heat of his skin, the pulse in his neck, and I tilted my mouth toward his ear.

"I said no to the date," I told him.

I heard him take a breath. He put his hand on the back of my neck, under my hair. Then he stroked slowly up the side of my neck, his skin gentle on mine, moving up beneath my ear until his palm cupped my jaw.

Against his neck, I closed my eyes. Andrew had never touched me before. It felt so good I wanted to cry. I never wanted it to stop.

He kept his hand there, and we stayed that way for a long moment. It was an embrace, almost. Or as close as either of us was willing to get.

Then Andrew turned his head so his lips were against my ear, his breath against my neck.

"Tessa," he said. "Go home."

SEVENTEEN

Andrew

THURSDAY. The routine of my fucking life. Get up, work out, shower. Dress. Today the housekeepers came, and when they were finished I ran two loads of laundry and answered the door to Tessa's air conditioner repair crew, who got her key from me and started work at her house. I turned on my across-the-street feed and kept an eye on it.

Today was doctor visit day, and Dr. Arnaud showed up just after one. He was a black man in his mid-fifties with close-cropped hair, wearing a comfortable short-sleeved button-down shirt and khakis. It was a casual outfit, but he still managed to look like a man who was not only working, but smarter than anyone else in the room.

He took my blood pressure, checked my heart and lungs, and asked me questions. Except for the legs, I was probably Dr. Arnaud's healthiest patient; I didn't have anything else physically wrong with me. His semi-regular visits were primarily about the meds I was on.

The suicide attempts meant I was depressed, of course. There was anxiety in the mix, as well as PTSD from the accident. They tried different drugs that were meant to help regenerate my nerves, though none of them had worked so far and I was off them at the moment. Medicinal weed jacked up my anxiety and insomnia, so that was a no go. There were drugs for pain and for sleeping that I said no to. Still, my blood usually contained a mix of some kind of cocktail.

Like I'd told Tessa, it wasn't the chair. It was the man that was in it.

"Things are looking good," Dr. Arnaud said when we were finished. He was sitting on my sofa, writing out notes and a couple of prescription renewals. "You're in prime shape, Andrew, so much so that I'm not sure why I need to keep coming here. You could come to the office sometime."

"And leave this paradise?" I asked, gesturing around me.

"Ah, the sarcasm. Still in full effect, I see."

"It's all I've got."

"Is that so?" He paused his scribbling to point his pen at my monitor feed. "You keep looking at that shot of the house across the street."

"My neighbor is getting her air conditioning fixed while she's out, and I promised her I'd keep an eye on it."

"Isn't your neighbor an elderly lady?"

I hate talking to people, but when you see the same people enough times, a few things inevitably slip out. "The elderly lady died and her granddaughter moved in."

Dr. Arnaud blinked his dark brown eyes twice at me, and basically saw everything inside me like an X-ray. "The granddaughter is pretty," he said, and it wasn't a question.

I scratched my beard. I was going to trim it as soon as he left. "No comment."

"So she is, then. What does she do for a living?"

"At the moment, she's at a photo shoot, modeling bras."

"Good lord, son." Dr. Arnaud rifled through his classy leather messenger bag. "Hold on a minute." He found a stack of brochures and picked out four of them. "Take these."

"What?" I took them and looked at them. "You have got to be fucking kidding me."

Spinal Cord Injury, Sex, and You.

Yes, You Can Still Have Satisfying Sex!

Couples Intimacy After SCI

26 Positions To Try

"Give them a read," Dr. Arnaud said. "You might find them interesting."

"Why is everyone so interested in my sex life? And do you just carry these around with you?" I flipped to the last one. "*Twenty-six* positions?"

"I'm a doctor, so I carry a lot of things with me. And yes, twenty-six positions. You can try some with your bra model."

"For fuck's sake. She isn't my bra model. And I'm probably the most sexually frustrated patient you've ever had, but this is still a bit much."

"Sexual frustration isn't healthy," Dr. Arnaud said without batting an eye. "As your doctor, I don't recommend it. Actually, if you could alleviate it, you might be able to get off some of these meds."

I glared at him. But I didn't give back the brochures.

"Okay, that was a joke," Dr. Arnaud said, though he'd shown no sign of laughing. "Sexual activity does not actually alleviate depression, anxiety, or PTSD. However, healthy sexual habits release endorphins and raise dopamine levels in the brain. It's good for you. There's no reason you can't have a healthy sex life, Andrew. I'll leave you some condoms."

"I don't need condoms."

He gave me a stern look. "Believe me, you do. As your doctor, I won't hear otherwise."

"No, I mean—"

"I know what you meant, and I'm not buying that either. Look, I treat a lot of patients with SCI. It's my specialty. The healthiest ones find a way to have regular sex, and some of them are married. With kids, even." He took some packets out of his magical bag. "Though it's a bit early for kids if you've just met this bra model, so as I say, here are some condoms."

There was movement on my security feed, and I saw a car pulling into my driveway. A familiar car. Nick had texted me earlier, saying they had landed safely and were home.

"Shit, my brother is here," I said. "You have to leave." I looked at the brochures in my hand, the condoms on the table. "Oh, Jesus."

Dr. Arnaud was pulling a small bottle from his messenger bag. "I have some lubricant, too. It's probably going to be helpful."

"What? Give me that." I gathered up the brochures, the condoms, the bottle. "You carry lube around, too? What the hell, doc? You're worse than Donna the wellness therapist. You sure you don't want to put some crystals around my house?"

"Crystals are not scientifically proven," Dr. Arnaud said, finally closing his goddamned bag and standing up. "Lubricant, however, is."

"For Christ's sake, get out of here already."

He left while I wheeled quickly to my bedroom and dumped the loot into the drawer of my bedside table. He must have let Nick in my door while he was exiting, because next I heard a familiar growly voice: "Hey fuckface, we're back. Where are you?"

I slammed the door and wheeled back out to the living room. Nick was standing there in his usual worn jeans and tee. He had Evie with him, her red hair tied up in a messy ponytail, a smile on her face at the sight of me. They both looked tan, happy, relaxed, and, yes, completely sexually satisfied after two weeks of nonstop, uninterrupted banging.

Jesus. Seven years of perfectly content celibacy, and all I could think about anymore was sex.

"Andrew!" Evie said, coming forward. She was wearing a pretty sundress. She leaned forward and kissed my cheek. She smelled like suntan lotion and happiness.

Fuck, it was hard to be in a bad mood when Evie was around. "I see you're still married to my brother," I said to her. "If you're in distress, blink twice."

"Ha ha," she said wryly. "Here, I brought you a present."

She dropped a gift bag in my lap, and I opened it. Inside was a statuette of a Hawaiian girl in a grass skirt and coconut bra—classic kitsch. I pressed the button on the base and she started to gyrate, her hips circling mechanically as a few notes of tinny music played. "Welcome to Hawaii!" came a high-pitched recorded voice as the girl danced. "Welcome to Hawaii!"

I sighed and turned it off. It really was hard to be in a bad mood when Evie was around.

"What did Dr. Arnaud say?" Nick asked, dropping onto the sofa.

"He said that after two weeks without you here, I'm healthier than ever," I replied. "I should probably move to Montana."

"Did you work on Lightning Man?"

"A little bit."

Nick's eyebrows went up. I usually worked on Lightning Man for hours a day, escaping into the comic-book world I loved so much. I'd still done a good amount of work in two weeks, but I'd been distracted by Tessa.

"So that's it?" Nick said. "You just hung out here and worked?"

"What?" I was distracted again. The air conditioning guys were finished across the street. I watched the feed as they locked Tessa's door and put her key in her mailbox, like I'd told them to. I noted the time. I'd offered to send Tessa updates, but she told me that models whose phones are constantly pinging on set look unprofessional. Instead she'd call me when she had a break.

Nick repeated himself. "I said, nothing happened while we were gone? Nothing at all?"

I pulled my gaze from the security feed and looked at him. Even though he was sort of scowling at me, he looked happy and relaxed.

It was good to see my brother. He was bossy and rude and he gave a shit about me, even when I was being a dick. The push and pull of his presence had been an essential part of my life. But he was married now, and I remembered the panic I'd felt the day he left, the fear that I had no idea how I would get through two weeks without him. And yet it was two weeks later, Nick was back, and here I was, just fine.

Was that a good thing or a bad thing? I had no fucking idea. Who was I if I didn't depend on Nick as my lifeline?

"No, nothing happened," I told him. "I don't have a very eventful life."

Nick glanced at Evie, and a knowing look went between them. The kind of married-people look I'd have to get used to for the rest of my life.

"That's bullshit," Nick said, looking back at me. "I already talked to Mom, and she says you have a girlfriend. Named Tessa."

EIGHTEEN

Tessa

I'D NEVER BEEN a comic book reader. I liked books—mostly thrillers and romances, and I'd read *The Thorn Birds* a dozen times. But comics had never been my thing.

Maybe it was because I'd never read *The Electric Adventures of Lightning Man.*

I was reading it now. Andrew had given me access to all of the issues online. I'd started with Volume 1, Issue 1 and read them on my phone, scrolling from panel to panel. I was some fifteen issues in now, and I'd never been more engrossed in anything in my life. Lightning Man was funny, fast-paced, and actually kind of moving. And the illustrations... my God. Andrew was so freaking talented, I was amazed by it over and over again.

"Hold on, Tessa. We need to adjust the fill light."

I stood in the middle of a stark, cold photo studio, wearing nothing but a bra and a pair of panties. This set was of matching violet lace. Cardi B was playing on the sound system, a strategically placed fan was lightly blowing my hair, and several people stood around the edges of the set: the photographer, the assistant, one of the execs from the lingerie company, the stylist. I had my makeup professionally done and I looked like a million bucks. It was a great gig. And as I stood there on autopilot, I kept thinking about whether Lightning Man was going to find the potion that would give him his powers back.

He'd lost his powers when Temptus had slipped a potion into his nighttime cup of tea. Thunder Boy and Judy Gravity had made another potion to restore them, but they'd had to hide the vial in the lab when Temptus's goons had broken in. Now Thunder Boy and Judy were kidnapped, tied up in a warehouse while Lightning Man searched for the potion. What was going to happen next?

"Okay, Tessa, we're back in action. A little to the left, please."

The stylist came onto the set and adjusted my bra strap. You'd think something as simple as a bra and underwear wouldn't need a stylist. You'd be surprised.

I did my thing, giving the camera a few different angles to choose from as the photographer snapped away. I knew exactly how to place my shoulders, what angle to tilt my chin, how to position my thighs to the most flattering effect. As I did it I thought about Lightning Man again.

Not just the story and the illustrations, which were amazing. The idea of it. Andrew and Nick had created something different, something creative and cool. Something brave.

They'd decided to do what they really wanted and said *fuck it, let's try.*

And as I stood there, showing off my tits, I couldn't get that out of my head.

"Perfect! Thirty minute break."

There was lunch served on a side table, but I wasn't going to have any. I had to shoot for another hour after this, and I couldn't have stomach bloat. So I put on a robe and drank a glass of lemon water as I sat in a chair and texted Andrew.

Tessa: What's happening with the air conditioning guys?

Andrew: They're done. How is the shoot?

Tessa: It's fine. I have a question.

Andrew: Why am I not surprised?

Tessa: How did you and Nick start Lightning Man?

Andrew: It was after my accident. Nick spent a lot of time at the hospital with me. We had to do something besides stare at each other and drive each other crazy.

Tessa: So you just started telling stories?

Andrew: Something like that. Why?

Tessa: Weren't you afraid your stories or your drawings wouldn't be good enough? That they'd suck?

Andrew: Is this a weird way of telling me you don't like my comics?

Tessa: No. They're brilliant. Which your giant ego already knows.

Andrew: My giant ego appreciates the compliment.

Tessa: But you didn't KNOW it was going to be great at first.

Andrew: No. But it was better than dying. By the way, Nick is back from his honeymoon. He talked to our mother. Now he thinks you're my girlfriend, and he also doesn't like you.

Tessa: Oh my God. Wear one FUCK shirt and get a permanent bad reputation.

Andrew: There goes the neighborhood.

Tessa: What can I do to impress him?

Andrew: You don't need to impress him because you're not actually my girlfriend.

Tessa: Right. Like Judy Gravity isn't ACTUALLY Lightning Man's girlfriend.

Andrew: She isn't.

Tessa: She so is.

Andrew: No, she isn't.

Tessa: They're calling me. Off to show the girls for money, then to Miller's for my shift. And she is.

Andrew: Damn it, Tessa.

<hr>

ON THE SAME day my air conditioner was fixed, the heat was finally breaking. As I worked my evening shift at Miller's, the wind kicked up and there was a dark bank of clouds on the far horizon. I watched them as I stood in the back alley on my break, feeling the hot, angry wind throw dirt onto my skin. My bobbed hair flew upward as the air swirled.

"Looks like it might storm," Nate said when he came out to join me, pulling a cigarette from the pack in his pocket.

I nodded. There seemed to be no lingering repercussions from my turning down my boss for a date, though I noticed him looking me up and down more often than I was comfortable with. And he tended to join me on my breaks, like now. "I guess it might," I said.

"About time the heat broke." He lit a cigarette and offered me the pack. "Want one?"

"No, thanks. I don't smoke."

"I noticed that. Why do you come out here on your breaks, then?"

To be alone for twenty freaking minutes without having to talk to anyone. But that sounded bitchy, so I just shrugged my shoulders. "I need some fresh air."

"I get that," he said, taking a drag of his cigarette at the same time and obviously not getting the irony. "Are you still seeing that guy?"

I looked at him.

"When I asked you out, you said you were sort of seeing someone," he said. "Are you still seeing him?"

Was he for real? That was only days ago. I was glad now that I'd said no. "Yes, I am."

I thought of the moment when I'd put my cheek to Andrew's, felt his warmth, smelled his skin. It didn't matter that he'd told me to go home. I was still seeing someone.

"Yeah?" Nate said. "What does he do for a living?"

What did it matter? "He's an illustrator and a programmer."

Nate's expression went hard, and I realized because it was some kind of comparison game, a dick-measuring contest. "Yeah, he sounds like a real winner," he said. "Some guys have all the luck."

I stared at him, shocked. I thought of Andrew getting in that car seven years ago, cocky and gorgeous and drunk. I thought of the photo I'd seen of the car smashed into the guardrail, the sickening way the metal was twisted. For the first time I let myself think of what it was like, really like, for him to live through that. Of how it would damage every part of a normal person. Of the kind of strength it took for him to get through it. "He isn't lucky," I said to Nate. "I have to go in now."

I went back to my shift, but something was bothering me. Something that crawled through the back of my mind as I wiped counters and washed glasses, my feet sore and my back aching. It circled my thoughts as I ate dinner, finally putting some food in my stomach after skipping lunch and working a long day. When I finished at one in the morning, I was exhausted and out of sorts.

It was raining. I drove home as huge, warm drops fell from the sky, making loud smacks on my windshield. By the time I pulled into my driveway the rain was coming down so hard I could barely see. I turned off the ignition and looked across the street.

Andrew's house was dark. Of course it was; he was probably

asleep. And still I got out of my car, letting the rain hit me as I walked across the road to his front porch, pulling out my phone.

He answered on the first ring, so he must not have been asleep after all. "Tessa, what are you doing on my porch?" he said.

I stepped in front of his door, in full view of his security camera. "Can you let me in?" I asked, looking up into the lens.

"Why?"

"I want to ask you a question."

He must have heard something in my voice, because his own voice grew tense. "Tessa, I'm going to bed."

"What does *it was better than dying* mean?"

Now he was defensive, on full alert. "What?"

"You said that doing the Lightning Man comics was better than dying. What did that mean?"

The briefest pause—barely a second, but I caught it. "It means I was in an accident that almost killed me."

"But you started doing the comics after the accident. And you said that doing them was better than dying."

He sounded harsh and more tired than anyone could possibly be. "Tessa, go home."

"Let me in."

"God, you are fucking insane. You never take a hint, do you? *Go home.*"

I swiped my wet hair back from my face. I was under the overhang of his porch, but I'd gotten soaked on my way across the street. Lightning flashed, followed by a roll of thunder. At one in the morning, there was no one else on the street. "Did you try to kill yourself?" I shouted over the thunder. "Is that what that means? Because I know what that feels like."

"You don't know anything about what I feel," Andrew said. "Not the first fucking thing."

"I know what it feels like to think you're worthless. To be lost.

To believe that no one could ever want you or love you, that no one will ever love you. To feel like you don't have anyone in your world and you never will. That you'll always be alone, and it looks so long and hard that you don't know what the point of it is."

"Do you?" Andrew said, his voice raw through the phone. He was angry now, and I welcomed it. It matched my own emotion. "Do you know what it feels like for me to watch you walk out my fucking door every day? To know that some guy is going to come on to you while I sit here, and one day you're going to say yes? And then you'll be gone, Tessa. Like everyone else."

I banged a fist on his door. "Andrew, let me in!"

"No."

I banged again. "I spent three weeks in a mental hospital when I was seventeen," I shouted into the phone. "I had a breakdown, okay? I couldn't handle anything anymore."

NINETEEN

Tessa

HE LET ME IN.

The house was dark. When I closed the front door behind me, the lock clicked. A voice from down the corridor said, "Back here."

I stepped through the living room to the hall. There was a dim slice of light coming from the bedroom.

I took a step, and my feet squelched. I kicked off my soaked sandals and walked, dripping, down the hall toward the slice of light. I could feel my T-shirt clinging to my body, the ends of my hair dripping water down my neck. I felt heat pulsing through me —adrenaline, embarrassment, lust—and shivers on my skin. I felt terrified and ecstatic and alive.

He hadn't said anything about what I'd just told him. Not a word. But this was Andrew. He didn't have to say it. *I'm sorry, that's too bad, I hope you're okay, have you tried therapy?* No. The things people struggled to say would sound ridiculous coming from Andrew. He didn't have to say a fucking thing.

At the bedroom doorway, I stopped. I was familiar with Andrew's bedroom, but it looked different tonight. The only light was from a bedside lamp; the blinds were shut. I could hear rain lashing the windows and thunder rolling overhead. Except for the sound of the storm, it was quiet.

Andrew's chair was pushed to the foot of the bed, empty. Andrew sat on the edge of the bed with the covers pulled back behind him. I'd obviously caught him just as he'd maneuvered himself into bed, getting ready to get under the covers. He was wearing nothing but boxer shorts.

I took a minute to take him in. His shoulders were sleek and muscled, his arms like marble as his hands braced against the bed on either side of his hips. He had a short dusting of dark hair on his chest, over his pectorals and down the perfect line of his stomach. His chest was wide and strong, his abs and his waist perfect. I could even see hard muscles lining the sides of his ribcage.

His thighs were sleek and strong, not bulky. His calves were thin. He was barefoot, his feet resting limply against the bedside rug.

I raised my gaze back to his shoulders, his gorgeous collarbones, and then his face. He had trimmed his beard so it was sleek to his jawline. His dark hair was brushed back from his forehead. His beautiful mouth was set. And his eyes watched me with wariness tinged with hurt and anger and lust.

I knew he'd looked me up and down, just as I had him. I knew my shirt was wet and my nipples were hard, that my chest was rising and falling, that my cheeks were flushed. I liked that he'd seen all of that. I felt naked in front of him anyway.

He was tense as he sat there looking at me, his muscles bunching, his hands gripping the edge of the mattress. Even his knuckles were sexy.

"That was the truth?" he asked me, his voice rough.

He meant the confession I'd just given him. "Yes," I said.

There was no joking now, no back-and-forth banter. The Andrew who used his wits as a defense, who would say something about how I must be crazy to hang out with him, was gone tonight. There was only this Andrew, who had been pulled out of that twisted car and gone into the darkness, who had put himself back together using the only tools he had. Who was still putting himself back together, day after day.

Lightning flashed through the blinds, and thunder rolled. Still, Andrew's gaze held mine. "You can't fix this," he said in his rough voice, motioning to his legs. "Do you understand that? I'm not a project or a broken piece of furniture. You can't fix it. I will always be like this. Always. You can't fix me."

I nodded. "I can't fix myself, either," I said.

"You can," Andrew replied. "You will. And then you'll leave."

I could have denied it, but he wouldn't have believed me. I knew what I was; I was strong, and I was tough, but I was broken. I wasn't nice. I wasn't normal. I wasn't going to get married and have babies and have a nice life. I was always going to be thinking around the next corner, tangling things up in my head, cutting people with my sharp edges. It was how I was, and nothing was ever going to make me soft and sweet and gentle. I couldn't fix myself; the only thing I could do was learn to like myself. It was something I'd started on the day I'd gone to his door with a cake in my hands.

And I wasn't going to leave. But Andrew wouldn't believe a string of arguments and words. The only thing that mattered to him was action.

So I reached for the hem of my T-shirt and pulled it off over my head.

Andrew breathed in and closed his eyes as if I was hurting

him. He breathed out again as I unzipped my jeans and pushed them down my hips, peeling them off. They made a damp sound as they hit the floor.

He opened his eyes again. I was in nothing but a bra and panties. I reached behind my back, unclasped the bra, and tossed it away.

"Christ," he said softly, under his breath. I wasn't sure he even knew he'd said it.

I walked toward the bed. I braced myself with a hand on his bare shoulder—his skin was smooth and warm under my palm—and swung a leg over his lap as if I was getting in a saddle. I lowered myself onto his thighs and slid forward, my inner thighs against his hips. I settled myself against him, my bare breasts brushing his chest, and ran my hands down the smooth muscles of his arms.

"I'm cold," I said, my voice raw.

He took another breath, his body stiff for a moment, and then he relaxed just a little as my ass settled onto his thighs. He seemed to be breathing me in. I knew I was doing the same to him; he smelled like he always did, vital and clean and tangy, the smell of a man. The smell of a man I wanted.

He lifted his chin and looked at me. His hands left the mattress and his palms came to my waist, smoothing down over my hips, then up again. He didn't grab my ass or my tits; instead he ran his hands up the sides of my ribcage, then to my back as I shivered in his lap, my nipples hard against him. I arched a little in pleasure as he stroked my back, up my shoulder blades, both of us melting into each other piece by piece.

Then he moved his hand up to the back of my neck, his fingers in my hair. He pulled me down to him and kissed me.

Thunder crashed again, and I parted my lips. He angled my head and kissed me deeply, his taste in my mouth, and as I throbbed at his touch I realized something: Andrew was experienced. I didn't know what he'd been doing since the accident, but the man who was kissing me had definitely done it before. And he was very, very good at it.

His hands were good, too. Big and warm and confident, touching me in a way that was reverent and hot at the same time. I'd had too many bad dates in my life, too many unsatisfying makeout sessions with guys who tasted like tequila shots and thought that pinching my nipples through my shirt was a sexy move. I'd had too much sex that was a few minutes of nothing with only one of us getting off. Andrew's hands were like magic, moving over my skin like every inch of it was important. He slid one palm down and cupped my breast, and even though I'd spent most of my day standing nearly naked in front of strangers, for the first time I felt like the sexiest woman alive.

I slid my tongue into his mouth, and he made a sound that was almost like pain. The muscles in his shoulders were tense as steel, his breathing shallow. I broke the kiss but I kept my mouth close to his as I stroked my thumbs over his perfect cheekbones and his soft beard.

"Andrew," I said, "tell me the truth. Have you done this since the accident?"

He flinched a little under my fingertips, the slightest wince. His shoulders didn't soften. "Do not," he said, his voice hoarse, "do not use that as an excuse. Not now. Not ever."

An excuse for what? To pity him? To treat him differently? To leave?

No, he wouldn't want excuses. God, the raw courage of him. I'd never seen anyone so fucking brave.

I put my hand over his where it cupped my breast. I found his other hand and put it on my other breast, my fingers over his. I leaned in and kissed him, brushing my mouth over his soft lips. "No excuses," I said.

"Good," he said. His shoulders eased just a little, and he

leaned in and whispered in my ear, as if telling me a secret. "I can smell you."

The breath exhaled out of me. He probably could smell me— I was only wearing a scrap of fabric, and I was wet. And the words made me wetter. My hands tightened over his. "Touch me," I begged him.

"Lie down," he said.

Reluctantly, I slid off his lap and onto the bed. I scooted over as he took a second to arrange himself, pulling his legs up onto the mattress. He did it quickly, almost gracefully, at ease with himself, and for a second the thought went through my head that I didn't know *exactly* how this would happen. The position wouldn't be the same as it was with other men. There might even be some improvisation. Because Andrew wasn't like other men.

He was better.

I lay on my back, and then he was next to me, balanced on his hip, leaning over me. He braced himself on one gorgeous, muscled arm. He looked down at me, searching my face with his dark eyes.

"I'm not going to say it," he said. "I'm not going to ask it."

"Then don't," I said. I ran a hand down his chest, fascinated by the feel of it, the heat of his skin, the light whorls of hair. "We've done enough talking for a while, don't you think?"

For the first time, the ghost of a smile touched the corner of his mouth. Then he leaned down to me.

"You're right," he said. "No more talking."

TWENTY

Andrew

I WAS SHAKING.

Fucking shaking. I kept an iron grip on myself, trying not to let on. But I could feel the tremor in my muscles, the shaking urge in my hands. This was why I didn't do this—because it was too much. Too hard.

I'd had plenty of sex before the accident, with plenty of girlfriends. Not one of them had contacted me afterward. Not one.

I shouldn't be doing this. It was probably going to kill me.

And still I leaned in and kissed Tessa, feeling her sigh, tasting the sweet flavor of her mouth. Feeling how warm she was. *Touch me*, she'd said. The last thing I should be doing. The only thing I wanted to do.

I braced myself over her, lying on one hip and leaning in. I couldn't do what I wanted, which was climb between her legs and fuck her, but it was only a momentary frustration. I wasn't ready to be inside her yet anyway—that was too raw. Instead I ran my hands over her again, kissing her neck, testing the waters. Feeling what she liked, what made her sigh, what made her back arch. Feeling the contours of her amazing body. I hadn't let myself miss this—the feeling of a woman under my hands. I hadn't let myself think about it, because it was just one more thing that sent me into the dark.

But this wasn't any woman. This was Tessa, her blonde hair against my pillow, her blue eyes hazy with want, her skin warm against mine. She was here. She'd told me her darkest secret, the one she never told anyone, the one that lodged inside her all the time like a shard of broken glass. I knew what that felt like.

I ran my hand over her breast, my thumb brushing the nipple, and listened to her inhale. I kept my hand moving down over her ribcage, the perfect flat plane of her stomach. Everyone got to see this body, but who touched it properly? The way it deserved to be touched? Tessa hadn't let anyone touch her the right way in a long, long time—maybe ever. That much, I knew.

But she let me now. I stroked down past her belly button, then slid my fingers under the elastic of her panties. She let out a sigh and opened her long, gorgeous legs as I moved further down, pressing my fingers into her pussy.

She moaned aloud, closing her eyes and pressing her hips up into me. I let my forehead drop to her neck and concentrated, trying to do it right, trying not to come. She smelled like vanilla and woman-sweat and sex, like smoke from the bar where she'd worked her shift and the remains of the makeup she'd washed off after her shoot. She wasn't a dream girl or an illusion. She was just Tessa, and in that moment the only thing I wanted was to make her come.

I stroked her, pushing my fingertips into her, then up through her slick folds to her clit. Her hands dug into my biceps and her hips moved, grinding into me. "Oh, God," she said in a helpless voice.

I moved my fingers down again, into her, further this time. If Tessa had any inhibitions left, they were quickly disappearing. She gripped my arms harder—I was going to have marks—and ground herself onto my hand. "Andrew," she gasped.

"I like torturing you," I said against her skin.

"Don't," she said. "Don't—Oh, *fuck*."

I kept going, bringing my thumb into the mix, building her higher, higher. Watching her arch against my sheets, her eyes closed, her lips parted, her lashes against her cheeks.

When she came it spiraled out for a long time, moving through her body in waves as she cried out. My muscles were locked and stiff, my cock hard and hot against my belly, my breathing shallow. Tessa having an orgasm, brought on by me, was the hottest thing I'd ever seen.

Finally, she relaxed as my hand stilled. Her eyes opened and looked up at me. A smile touched her lips, sexy and powerful. "Your turn," she said, and her hand moved into my boxers, her fingers curling around my cock.

I made a surprised, undignified grunt. My arm gave out and I dropped to the bed, closing my eyes as sensation washed over me. Tessa put a palm against my shoulder and pushed me to my back, and it was her turn to lean over me, her hand moving up and down me.

It felt so good I thought I was going to fucking die. But first, I would come. Embarrassingly fast. I pressed my hands to the mattress and tried not to let it happen.

But it was inevitable. She stroked her hand up to the head, then down again, with just the right amount of pressure. Tessa's hand was stroking my cock, right now. My hips pushed up into her and my hands tangled into the sheets. Fuck, this was going to be fast.

"Jesus, Tessa, I'm going to come," I managed, because it was polite to at least warn her.

"That's the idea," she said. Then she bent down, the ends of her hair trailing against my stomach, pushed down the waist of my boxers, and slid her hot, wet mouth over my cock.

I came. It was almost painful, and it was certainly humiliating. I could have practically drowned her. That's how much of a fucking mess I was.

When I finished I ran my hands over my face, which was numb. I tried to breathe. One breath, and then another. My hands, I realized, were shaking. I had no way to stop it now.

I kept my eyes closed and felt Tessa kiss her way up my stomach, my chest. I couldn't speak. My mind was blank. I couldn't even form a single thought.

Tessa moved one of my hands away from my face and kissed my cheek. She didn't need me to speak; she didn't need me to do anything. She kissed down my cheek to my jawbone, up to my temple. She let her body relax against mine, pressed to my side. I took in a shuddering breath and tried to keep it together.

I opened my eyes as she rolled away from me. I thought she was going to get up, but she was only turning out the bedside lamp. She rolled back and lay against me again.

She fit against me so perfectly. My arm went around her, curling over her back. She lay her cheek against my shoulder.

We lay there without speaking, listening to each other breathe. We didn't seem to need words. She was right; we'd done enough talking for a while.

After a long time, I realized that we were lying in the dark, which I usually hated. But it didn't seem so bad.

Then I realized Tessa was asleep.

I had only a minute to think about it before I was gone into oblivion.

TWENTY-ONE

Tessa

I'VE ALWAYS BEEN a deep sleeper. When I'm out, I'm all the way out until I finally come back to consciousness. That must have been how Andrew got out of bed the next morning without me noticing.

It was early—just after seven, according to my phone, which was still in the pocket of my jeans on the floor. The rain had stopped in the night, the storm passing over. I pulled on my now-dry jeans and my T-shirt, ditching the bra, and crossed the hall to use the bathroom.

I felt...good. Really good. Rested and satisfied, though Andrew and I hadn't done the full range of things we could possibly do. We hadn't even started. And I still felt pretty freaking fantastic.

I came out of the bathroom and heard sounds from the other room in the hall. I'd peeked into this room before and knew it was a workout room. Andrew was doing his morning workout.

He was on his back on a weight bench, doing chest presses. I stood in the doorway and watched for a minute, not wanting to startle him.

He was wearing a black tee and gray sweatpants. His arms and chest flexed, his dark eyes fixed on a point on the ceiling. A drop of sweat rolled down his temple and into his hair.

He put the weight down on its rack and sat up, looking at me over his shoulder. His expression was careful, unreadable. "Morning," he said.

And I felt it—that little trickle of excitement, like champagne bubbles moving through my blood. The feeling of being with a guy I liked. Of being the focus of his attention, of having nothing else to look at but him. "Morning," I said.

He swiveled on the bench, moving his legs off and putting his feet on the ground. I was getting used to it now, how Andrew arranged himself. It wasn't weird or clumsy; it was just how he moved. I walked to the bench and sat next to him.

This was the moment when it might be awkward. I'd told him my rawest secret last night, and I knew his. We hadn't talked about it. We would, eventually, and it would be a dark conversation. We both had unresolved shit, and Andrew was convinced I was going to dump him. We'd had sort-of sex, we'd slept together, and we were both in uncharted territory. I should be fumbling around, making excuses and leaving. Instead I looked at him and thought, *Damn, girl, you got that. Get it again.*

"I have to go to work," I said, like a dope.

"Yeah," Andrew said. He scratched his chin slowly, his fingers rasping over his beard. He wasn't awkward either. He wasn't defensive or throwing quips at me. This was thoughtful Andrew, his face relaxed, his eyes focused on the wall as the super-intelligent thoughts went around in his head. I looked at his fingers and thought of how they'd touched me last night, how they'd made me come.

He'd had a lot of women, once upon a time. I saw that now. I could see the twenty-three-year old who had all the women he wanted.

But none of those women were here now. I got him all to myself.

"You're going to the photo shoot?" he asked, glancing at me.

I didn't want to think about taking my clothes off in front of a lot of people, but I said, "Yeah. It's the last day. Then I'm working a shift at Miller's."

He nodded. "You hungry?"

"I can't eat right before a shoot. I'll get coffee on the way. I'm going home to shower and change."

"Okay."

"I'm coming over later. After my shift."

He looked at me again, his eyes catching mine. Something flickered in his, and he said, "You sure?"

It was the one and only time he'd ask me, I knew. He was giving me an out. "I'm sure," I said.

He dropped his hand, still looking thoughtful. "Sex with me is going to be different," he said frankly.

"Okay," I said.

"I mean, I don't really know how it goes. I'm pretty sure I can make it good, but I'll have to figure a few things out. You need to be patient. It won't be like you're used to with other guys."

I couldn't help it. "You mean you'll call me afterward?" I said.

Andrew sighed, but he looked amused.

"Okay, seriously," I said. I reached out and put my hand on his arm, close to his wrist, wanting to feel his skin against mine. "Does sex with you involve your cock inside me?"

His face went still. "Tessa."

"Because I haven't had that yet and honestly, I'm pretty interested."

"Tessa."
I leaned in and kissed his cheek. "See you later."
When the door closed behind me, I was smiling.

TWENTY-TWO

Andrew

NICK and I were sitting in my living room, Nick on the sofa, me at my computer. Nick's dog, a ridiculous chihuahua named Scout, was on the sofa next to Nick, lying on her back, hoping he —or anyone—would rub her belly. Yes, my big, tough brother had a chihuahua, and he was actually attached to her. It was a long story.

Nick was jotting ideas down on a notepad. I was using my tablet to draw a panel for the latest Lightning Man comic.

"Okay, so he's saved Judy Gravity from the underworld," Nick said. "What next? They need to take on another mission."

I was drawing the underworld scene. Lightning Man was lifting a giant fiery boulder, looking for Judy beneath it. "Judy?" he called in the dialogue box. "Judy!"

"I called the venue for the comic convention," Nick said. "They say it's wheelchair accessible."

"No," I said.

We'd been over this once already. A big comic convention was coming to Detroit, a few hours' drive away. They'd contacted us and asked if we wanted to come—speak on a panel, meet readers, sign copies of Lightning Man.

Leave my house. Stay in a hotel. Talk to people. No.

"The hotel is accessible, too," Nick said.

I didn't look up from my drawing. "No."

"Too bad, dirtbag. You're going."

This was my brother's version of a pep talk. No wonder I was in therapy. "How would we get to Detroit?" I asked.

"How do you think? I'll drive."

I put my pen down and pressed the pad of my thumb into my eye socket, where a headache was suddenly starting. Driving was bad for me—very bad. Sitting in the passenger seat of a car made me think of the accident. Short trips to and from the hospital were hard enough; a few hours on the highway sounded like a nightmare. "You go without me," I said.

Nick patted Scout, who wiggled idiotically in happiness. "No way, asshat. We both go. It's an opportunity."

"No, it's a hellish dystopia."

Nick made a sound between a sigh and a growl. "For fuck's sake."

I thought about Tessa, how she'd looked this morning. Tousled and relaxed and beautiful, wearing last night's clothes. I calmed down a little, and the headache didn't throb as hard. I took a breath and looked at the panel I was drawing. "Judy!" Lightning Man was shouting.

I picked up the tablet pen and started filling in the hot coals and flames of the underworld. "I don't think Lightning Man and Judy Gravity should go on a mission," I said. "I think they should go on a date."

Nick picked up his notepad. "Judy isn't Lightning Man's girlfriend."

I drew Lightning Man's tortured expression as he looked for her. "You know, I think she is."

Nick put down his pad again and looked at me, ignoring Scout, who gazed at him worshipfully. I kept drawing.

"What?" I said finally, my eyes on the screen.

"You got laid," Nick said.

"I did not." Technically true. If you followed a very narrow definition of "laid."

"Fucking hell," Nick said. "You think I don't know what Laid Andrew looks like? I saw him enough times."

"Laid Andrew has no comment," I said, filling in Lightning Man's costume. "Neither does Un-Laid Andrew."

"I want to meet this woman," Nick said. "Tessa."

"Are you going to ask if she has honorable intentions toward me?"

"Can you be fucking serious for a minute? This is important."

I lowered my pen and turned to look at him. He was sitting up on the sofa, scowling at me.

"You don't think I'm serious?" I said.

"You don't know this woman," Nick said. "She just showed up. She could be anyone."

"Is it your mission to annoy the shit out of me today?" I asked him. "First I have to take a two-hour drive on the highway, and now any woman who likes me is up to something."

"I didn't say that."

The headache was starting again. Nick and I liked to insult each other, but we didn't fight like this. We usually just sat here, making up stupid stories for comics. That was what we'd done for seven years.

And then Nick had found Evie. And he got married. And now there was Tessa. Everything was fucking changing.

I'd had enough change in my life already. Way too much. Change made everything worse.

"You know what?" I said to Nick. "You're right. Don't worry about Tessa. I don't know how long she's going to be around."

"What does that mean?"

I raised my eyebrows. "It means it's a short-term relationship. You used to be pretty familiar with those."

He scowled harder.

"We're not getting married and having babies," I said. "She'll bail out after a while. In the meantime, I'm thirty fucking years old and the accident didn't lower my IQ, so relax."

Nick opened his mouth, probably to argue some more, but there was a knock on my front door. I checked the security feed. It was Evie. She'd left us to run some errands while we worked, and now she was back. I let her in.

"Hey," she said, coming into the room and pushing her sunglasses up on her head. Scout jumped off the sofa, wagging her whole body at Evie in greeting, and then jumped back up, adoring Nick again. Evie's smile faltered a little when she caught the vibe between Nick and me.

"Um," she said, "are you guys done?"

"We're done," Nick said, picking up his notebook and pencil and putting them in his bag. His tone was calm.

"Sure," I said. "We're done."

"Okay. This was on your porch." Evie scooped up Scout and held out a piece of paper to me. I took it. It was a flyer advertising the neighborhood barbecue on Saturday. "Games for the kids!" it said, in Comic Sans font, the paper printed at the local Kinko's. "Burgers! Dogs! Come have fun and meet your neighbors!"

I tossed the flyer aside. Nick and Evie left, and I wheeled to the kitchen to get myself a sandwich. It was physiotherapy day, and my head hurt like hell.

TWENTY-THREE

Tessa

I HAD BEEN to dozens of casting calls in my career. I'd made sacrifices. I'd stood in many studios just like this one, smiling for the camera. Modeling was my dream and my career.

Today I didn't want to do any of it.

I was standing in my underwear, doing the easiest job in the world, and I didn't really want to be here. It was cold, and I was hungry because I'd skipped breakfast for black coffee in order to look thin. But aside from that, there was something just... off. I didn't feel the happiness I usually felt doing this.

Honestly, I wanted to be wearing sweats and a stretched-out T-shirt, lounging on Andrew Mason's sofa, listening to him shoot barbs at me. Eating his pickles. I itched to text him every time we had a pause, but I refrained. It would seem clingy, like I was feeling sappy about him. He'd probably hate it.

Besides, I wasn't feeling sappy about him. At all.

Last night was good. Really, really good. But I didn't do relationships, and neither did he. We had a thing. It was a good thing, but it was just a thing. Not a sappy, messy commitment.

We were on the final few products for the catalog, which included a strapless bra and one with criss-crossed straps. When we finally took a break, I sipped my lemon water and stared at my phone, pondering for the thousandth time whether I should text Andrew. As I was moping over it, the phone rang in my hand.

It was my mother. I did a quick calculation: It was around noon in Colorado. What the hell was she calling me for?

"Hey Mom," I said when I answered, trying not to sound put out.

"I can't believe you," my mother said.

I frowned. "What are you talking about?"

"The money." My mother usually had a chill hippie attitude, but she could get petty and angry. Right now she was both. "You're just going to keep it, aren't you? You're not going to share any of it with me."

"What money?"

She made a disbelieving sound. "You're going to pretend you don't know about the money? I talked to the lawyer, Tessa. He said he sent you a letter about it."

The lawyer had sent me a letter? If it had come to my grandmother's house, I hadn't seen it. But then again, I hadn't been home yesterday. I'd worked all day and all night, then I'd stayed the night at Andrew's. "Wait a minute," I said to Mom. "You're saying that aside from the house, Grandma left me money?"

"*All* of her money," Mom said. "Including the money left to her when my father died and she got a life insurance payout. She left you everything, and she didn't leave any of it to her own daughter."

I blinked in shock. I realized I was standing in the dressing room in my underwear, and I grabbed a robe and pulled it on, wrapping it around me. "I didn't know about the money, Mom," I said. "I swear I didn't."

"Well," she said, only half believing me, "I'm a little short right now, and I need funds. If you could send some, it would be great. Considering it's really both of our inheritance."

I opened my mouth, and the words that were going to come out were the ones without thinking: *Yes Mom, sure, of course you're right.* The words were right there on my tongue. And then I stopped myself.

I hadn't known my grandmother. I'd never talked to her. I didn't know her before she died. Whose fault was that? My mother's, for sure. Maybe my grandmother's, too. Maybe all three of us took some of the blame.

The point was, I didn't have the chance to ask what my grandmother was thinking. But instead of that, her will left a pretty clear message.

"Grandma didn't want you to have her money," I told Mom. "She wanted me to have it."

"Don't be silly, Tessa. Of course my mother wanted me to have some of that money."

"Then why didn't she leave it to you in the will?"

"We were having a bit of an argument, that's all. We weren't getting along."

"Mom, you weren't getting along with Grandma for *twenty-seven years.*"

"She had a closed mind," Mom said. "She didn't understand your father and me."

I thought about my grandmother in that house, watching her pregnant nineteen-year-old daughter drive away with her boyfriend forever, telling her to fuck off as she went. "Maybe she didn't understand, but probably because she was worried about you. She didn't want you to make a mistake."

"So you're taking sides, then?"

Again, the words tried to come out: *No, of course not, I'll do what you want, sorry.* But I could feel a current of something stubborn and resistant in my blood. Maybe it was anger; maybe it was the spirit of my grandma, telling me what her wishes were. "So you left your mom, you cut her out of your life, you kept her granddaughter away from her, and now you think she owes you her money?" I said. "I think maybe she'd disagree."

Mom was starting to get angry now. "I can't believe you're saying this. You don't understand anything."

"How many times did she call you, Mom?" I said. "How many times did she beg to have a relationship with you again over the last twenty-seven years? And a relationship with me?"

Mom was silent, which answered my question.

"A dozen?" I asked her. "A hundred? You were her only child, and I was her only grandchild, and you made the decision to cut us off. *You* did that. You didn't even go to the funeral when your dad died. Grandma lived the rest of her life a lonely old lady, and she died alone. And now you think you should get her money."

"I don't know what's happened to you," Mom said. "I didn't raise you to be disrespectful."

"You didn't raise me at all." The crew at the other end of the studio could probably hear me; they were glancing at me uneasily. I didn't care. The words came out hot and unstoppable, like lava. "You left me to fend for myself while creeps leered at me as soon as I turned thirteen. You never came to a single school event or parent-teacher meeting. I was barely even supervised most of the time—I just ran around free. Anything could have happened to me. And when I was suicidal at seventeen, I went to the hospital and asked for help alone. You weren't even in the country."

"So that's it," Mom said. "You're going to blame me for all of your problems."

Something shot through my blood like fire, and I realized it was anger. Pure rage. When I'd left the hospital after three weeks of treatment, no longer a danger to myself, Mom had argued against me getting therapy or medication. She'd said they "weren't natural," and that I just needed to "work through" my problems. As if I'd imagined it all. As if none of those feelings were real.

So I'd left home. I'd headed for L.A. to try for an acting and modeling career. And I had gotten therapy, when I could afford it—which was rarely. I'd built my life, built myself, all alone, out of nothing. No wonder the person I'd built was a fucking mess.

"I'm taking Grandma's money," I told Mom. "I'm going to go to nursing school. I'm going to build a life for myself. I think that's what she wanted."

"Oh, Tessa." Mom sounded exasperated. "For God's sake, you can't be a nurse."

"Why not?"

"It just isn't you."

They were motioning for me to come back to the set, wind up the shoot. The break was over. "You mean I'm not smart enough," I said. "You don't think I can do it."

"It isn't fair," Mom said. "You're going to waste that money."

I felt like she'd slapped me. Even after all of the years, with how well I knew my mother, it still hurt, how selfish she was. How blind she was to the pain she caused everyone. "Then I guess I'll waste the money," I said. "Bye, Mom."

I hung up. I turned off my phone.

Then I dropped my robe and said, "Let's go."

TWENTY-FOUR

Andrew

I WAS LYING on my sofa, reading comics. Okay, to be honest, I was drifting off—getting laid for the first time in seven years last night had been pretty eventful, and Jon had practically tortured me in my physio session today, making me work the functioning muscles in my legs until they screamed. "Someday they're going to have a way for you to walk again, man," he'd said with perfect confidence. "Science is moving fast. Your legs have to be ready."

So I was dozing, imagining I could actually feel some of the pain below my knees, when my phone rang. I knocked the comic off my chest and saw that it was Tessa. "What's up?" I asked when I answered.

"Were you asleep?" she asked. "Sorry."

"It's fine." I looked at the time: six o'clock. She should be working her shift at Miller's right now. "Is something wrong?"

"No. Maybe? Yes. I think? I'm coming over."

"What?" I sat up and checked the security feed. Sure enough,

Tessa was coming out of her front door across the street, holding the phone to her ear, instead of pouring drinks at Miller's. "Why aren't you at work?" I asked her, running a hand through my hair.

"It's a long story." I watched her lock her door and start across the street. She was wearing a long sundress that went all the way down to her ankles, but I could still see how her body moved under the loose fabric. She had a bag over her shoulder. "I kind of don't work at Miller's anymore."

"Kind of?"

"Okay, I completely don't work there anymore. I got fired. It's been kind of a crazy day."

"All right," I said. "Come in."

I buzzed her in and moved my feet to the floor so I wasn't hogging the sofa. Tessa came in, bringing the smell of sweet summer air with her. She'd had a shower and scrubbed her makeup off, and her hair was damp. Her eyes were a little wild. She was frazzled.

She dropped down onto the sofa next to me and smiled. "Hi."

"Hi," I said. "You don't look upset that you got fired."

"I'm not, really." She bit her lip. "Actually, my boss asked me out again, and when I said no, he fired me. I told him he was an asshole, and I left."

I stared at her. "Your boss fired you because you wouldn't date him?"

"Pretty much. He also called me a cunt while I walked out the door."

I felt my hands curl into the fabric of the sofa. "He called you what? I'll go punch his fucking teeth in." I didn't know how I would do that, of course. I'd have to get over there first. Maybe I'd call a cab, or an Uber. I was willing to brave a car if it meant I could smash this guy's face.

Tessa smiled at me, a dreamy sort of smile. "You're awesome when you're angry, but he isn't worth the assault charge."

"He can't just do that," I ground out.

"He already did, but forget it. I'm not upset, I promise. I didn't want to work there anyway."

I remembered that today was the last day of the photo shoot, so she didn't have any more money coming in. "Are you going to get another job?"

"That's just the thing," Tessa said, opening her bag and pulling out papers. "I don't have to rush to get another job. Because I got these today."

She handed them to me, and I read them over. It was from Mrs. Welland's estate lawyer, informing Tessa that she had inherited funds from her grandmother. I looked at the number and blinked. "Holy shit, Tessa. Even after the taxes and the rest of it, this is a pretty good amount of money."

"I know. It won't set me up for life, but I can get by for a little while, don't you think?"

"Sure you can." I looked up at her, then remembered it was dinner time. She never ate at photo shoots. "Are you hungry? I'll get you a sandwich."

She watched me lever myself off the couch and into my chair with widened eyes. "Andrew, no. I can get it myself."

"Relax, I'll get it."

"Andrew."

I held up a hand. "Bea Arthur. Remember? You're being an ass. I can make sandwiches, despite the fact that I'm catastrophically infirm."

She slumped a little. "Sorry. And I love it when you use big words. Which reminds me, I actually came over here to have sex."

"I know, but now you have to wait for it." I wheeled to the kitchen. "Keep talking."

She kept talking as I made her sandwich, ugly mustard and all. She told me about the phone call from her mother, the argument over the money. Then, after getting fired from Miller's, she'd gone home and found the letter from the lawyer in the mailbox. She'd just gotten off the phone with him.

"So, that's it," she said as I put her sandwich, pickle, and ginger ale down in front of her. "My bills are paid for a while. Which is weird, because right before it happened I was thinking I'd like to do a job with my clothes on for a change."

I watched her inhale the sandwich—she was freaking starving—and said, "Nurses keep their clothes on. At least, the ones I know always do. You could use that money to go to nursing school."

She swallowed her last bite, looking troubled. "My mother says I'll fail and waste the money."

"Your mother sounds like she doesn't do much mothering, to be honest. I know the type well."

Tessa poked at the crumbs on her plate. "Andrew, I'm an underwear model and bartender. Do you think I'm smart enough to go to nursing school?"

"Yes," I said honestly. "I've spent a lot of time in hospitals, and I've met a lot of nurses. They're great people. Hardworking, dedicated, smart people. You're just as smart as any of them."

"Ugh." She let out a stressed-out sigh. "I've always wanted to do it, but now that it's actually possible, I'm pretty much terrified."

"You'll do great," I said.

She would. She'd work hard, and she'd be a great nurse. And then she'd meet a great guy, and I'd be left in the dust. But I wasn't going to think about that now.

Tessa leaned back on the sofa and looked at me, sweeping her gaze up and down. "So you feed me and pay me compliments. That's your plan to get me into bed?"

I steepled my fingers beneath my chin. "Mustard is part of my plan for seduction."

"And ginger ale."

"You've been ensnared in my web from the beginning. Admit it."

She smiled, a sexy smile, a little mysterious. "Or maybe it's you who has been ensnared in my web."

Was she kidding? Tessa could snap her fingers and I'd do anything she wanted. Literally anything. It was all I could do to keep up the pretense, not to let on.

"Enough about my problems," she said. She leaned forward on the sofa and put her elbows on the arms of my chair, looking up at me. "What do we do now?"

Our eyes locked, hers a shade of blue that made me think of the hot summer sky before a storm blew in. I felt a long, slow beat of fear, my old friend. *This is going to hurt.*

I pushed it away. I had a beautiful woman sitting right here, and she wanted to sleep with me. We both wanted it, and there was no reason to say no. What would the old Andrew Mason do?

I knew the answer to that. So I said, "Now you take your dress off and go to the bedroom, and I'll follow you."

She blinked once. Those perfect long lashes sweeping down, then up. This was the moment when she could say she couldn't do it, that she'd changed her mind, that she'd made a mistake.

But this wasn't just any woman. This was Tessa.

She smiled at me.

"Okay," she said.

TWENTY-FIVE

Tessa

ANDREW HAD SAID, this morning, that he thought he could make it good. He was right.

He kissed me for a long time first. A *long* time. Even though I was impatient, those kisses were like a drug, a balm. As he lay next to me, braced over me as he'd been last night, his mouth trailing warmly along my neck and up behind my ear, how did he know that was what I wanted? Someone to touch me like I mattered. I didn't matter to anyone in my life: not my mother, not the shallow people at the modeling gig, not my boss who saw me as a piece of ass he could fire. To Andrew, I fucking mattered. How had I been without him for this long?

He ran his hands—his big, warm, wonderful hands—over me, and I closed my eyes. Everything disappeared. There was just the two of us, in this room, right now. I was hot and giddy at the same time. *I get Andrew all to myself! Just me!* Part of me couldn't quite believe it was happening.

His hand slipped down between my legs, and I tangled my fingers in his hair. It was soft and clean and awesome. "I want to do this all night," I said as he kissed my jaw.

"That doesn't give me anxiety or anything," Andrew growled against my skin.

I reached down between us and rubbed my palm on his cock, smooth and hot in my hand. "No anxiety needed," I said.

His body tensed as I rubbed him. "Just let me get through one time, first, and then I'll see what I can do."

"Fine." I put a hand on his chest and gently pushed him back, climbing on top of him as he rolled on his back. Now I could see his fine abs, the vee of the muscles over his hips, his perfect chest with its dusting of dark hair. Even his collarbones were sexy. He was looking at me, too, as I sat atop him, his dark eyes traveling me up and down.

I only wanted Andrew looking at me anymore. His was the only gaze that mattered.

I adjusted myself on his hips. "See, this isn't so hard."

A muscle in his jaw twitched. "Yes, it is."

I leaned forward, braced my hands on either side of him, letting my breasts brush his chest. "Difficult, I mean. It isn't so difficult."

I brushed my mouth over his, and he kissed me back. Breaking the kiss, he opened the drawer of his nightstand and took out a condom. I kissed down his neck and his collarbones as he rolled it on.

I was glad we'd had our little dress rehearsal last night. Our bodies were already familiar with each other; I knew his scent and the way his hands felt. He put his palms on my hips and guided me as I lowered myself down on him. We both moaned.

"God, that feels good," I said as I lowered all the way down.

His hands tightened on my hips. "Don't talk dirty," he growled. "Don't moan like that. I'll fucking lose it."

I licked the lobe of his ear. "I can't help it. You're hot."

"Tessa—*Jesus*." He tensed again as I started moving on him, rolling my hips. I let my head fall forward to the side of his neck and I closed my eyes because it felt so, so freaking good. It was heaven. I moved my knees, taking him deeper, and he growled again.

This was definitely not awkward, or weird, or difficult. It was amazing.

Andrew moved his hand up under my hair, gently gripping the back of my head. "Tessa, I want to throw you down and fuck you," he said. "You know I do. I want to fuck you until you can't move."

Now he was the one talking dirty. "I don't care," I said. "Just make me feel good."

His hand slid between us, his finger stroking my clit as I moved, and I gasped as a shock of pleasure moved through me. I rocked my hips, hitting his finger again and again, and every time the pleasure built higher. I kept my eyes closed and let it happen.

The orgasm was the most natural thing in the world, pulsing through me and making me cry out. I bit my lip and buried my face in Andrew's neck as his hands gripped my hips again and his own hips flexed up into me. And I felt every muscle as he came, his head tilted back and his eyes closed, as if he hadn't felt pleasure like this for seven long years.

TWENTY-SIX

Andrew

"IT WAS A BAD YEAR, I GUESS," Tessa said.

It was night. I was sitting up in bed, relaxed against the pillows propped against the headboard, the blanket pulled up to my waist. Tessa was sitting cross-legged in the middle of the bed, wearing my T-shirt. She'd found ice cream in my freezer and sprinkled it with nuts, and she was digging in.

She'd offered me a bowl, but I wasn't hungry. I was happy just to watch her, the way her eyes went unfocused with pleasure as she took a spoonful. I was starting to get the idea that in her life outside my house, her life as a model, Tessa didn't eat very much. Here, she was happy to clean out my fridge and my cupboards, which was fine with me.

"A bad year?" I said.

She took another spoonful. "Okay, fine, all of my teenage years were bad. And before that, so was my childhood." She looked thoughtful. "I always told myself it wasn't bad, because I wasn't abused or anything. But do you know why I wasn't abused? Because I got into scary situations all alone early in life, and I lucked my way out of them. By thirteen I knew how to spot a creepy guy or a bad situation. Those aren't things a thirteen-year-old should know."

"They aren't," I said.

"My father left when I was six," Tessa said. "His entire method of parenting was 'everyone should do their own thing.' Which is stupid when you're dealing with a little kid. But of course, when he left and picked up with another girl, he got to say it was because he was doing his own thing. My mom went on to other boyfriends after him. You know how some single parents really worry about dating, about how the person they're seeing will affect their kid? That wasn't her."

"Jesus," I said. "Terrible things could have happened to you."

"I know. A few of her boyfriends were creepy, but none of them lasted very long. I figured out how not to be alone with any of them, ever—even the nice ones. Because you never knew. As you may have gathered, I don't trust people." She glanced at me. "Am I talking too much?"

"Tessa," I said, "literally the only thing I want to fucking do right now is listen to you talk."

She lowered her bowl and spoon for a second. "Sometimes you say the nicest things," she said. "I don't even think you know you do it."

"Just keep talking, okay?"

She paused, then nodded. "I went off the rails as a teenager," she said. "I was the textbook definition of running with the wrong crowd. I hung out with people who partied and did all kinds of drugs. I tried all of them sooner or later. I blacked out more times than I could count. I lost my virginity in the backseat of a smelly truck to a guy who was twenty-five. I was so drunk I only half remember it. I had no curfew, and my mother never asked when I was going to be home. I thought I didn't matter. I hated myself."

My hands were clenched in the sheets, my heart pounding. I may be a mess now, but my teenage years had been fucking great. Sure, our parents pretty much ignored Nick and me, but otherwise we were rich, good-looking guys who liked to have fun. I'd lost my virginity to my first girlfriend; we'd planned it for weeks. We were sober, and we tried to make it great for both of us. We both failed, but that was nobody's fault.

Before the accident, my life had been so, so fucking good. I had that.

"What happened?" I managed to ask.

Tessa shrugged. She stirred the ice cream in her bowl. "I got drunk and high more and more. I realized it was because I never wanted to be inside my own head, just me and my thoughts. I was spiraling. The people I hung out with weren't really my friends; the guys I slept with barely knew my name. My mother didn't care. I started to fixate on the idea that if I disappeared, it wouldn't matter. That people would be better off. And it sounded really good."

I closed my eyes for a second. I knew that feeling. But I stayed quiet and let her talk.

"Part of me, though, got scared," Tessa said. "Part of me didn't want to do it, but I didn't feel in control. So one night when I was seventeen I went to the emergency room of the closest hospital and told them I needed help or I was going to kill myself. I saw one doctor, then another. They recommended I spend some time in a rehab center. They tried to call my mother because I was a minor, but she was at a yoga retreat in Costa Rica and couldn't be reached. They let me go in anyway."

"Did it help?" I asked.

She nodded. "I was in for three weeks. It was mostly group therapy, and of course there were no drugs or alcohol. If we had more money, I could have gone somewhere nicer. But at least I learned that I wasn't alone, that there were people like me out there who were getting help. That the drugs and alcohol weren't helping. That if other people could get through it, then maybe I could, too." She took the last, melted bite, her mood seeming to cheer up again. "When I left, I packed my bags and moved to L.A. I got away from those people, from the girl I was. I got jobs and made my own money, and I tried to make something of myself as a model. I didn't really succeed, but at least I tried. And then my grandmother died. And here I am."

Something clicked. "What you went through—that's part of why you want to be a nurse."

"Yes, it is." She put her empty bowl on the bedside table. "It's stupid, right? Thinking you might be able to help someone some-day, the way you were helped. I should be more cynical."

"It isn't stupid," I said. It was fucking amazing. She was fucking amazing. Tough and smart and indestructible.

She looked at me. Her hair was still messed from the sex we'd had, and she was wearing my shirt. If there was ever a better sight in the universe, I'd never seen it. "So now you know about me," she said. "Which of us wins the screwed-up Olympics?"

"Still me," I said. "Definitely me."

"Okay, you're probably right. But do I win anything for second place?"

I thought about it. "You win complimentary access to my air conditioning and my kitchen. And the undeniable pleasure of my company."

Tessa sighed. "Those big words." She came forward on all fours and moved closer to me. "I like your company."

I could smell her—sex, shampoo, woman. I cupped the back of her head when she got close and kissed her, me sitting up, her on all fours. It got hot, fast. She tasted so incredibly good.

"Why me?" I asked her when we finally broke the kiss. "Of all the guys. Why me?"

"Some things are just fate," Tessa said. "Don't you think?"

I couldn't answer, because she kissed me again. I could taste ice cream on her tongue.

She slid her hand down my stomach and beneath the sheet, where I was getting hard again. She broke the kiss as she stroked me. "I bet I can think of something you haven't had in seven years," she said softly.

My voice was choked. "That isn't necessary."

"I think it is." She kissed her way down my chest, my stomach. Lower.

She was right, of course. Seven years.

We fixed that.

She told me it tasted better than ice cream.

TWENTY-SEVEN

Tessa

FOUR DAYS later I was the Millwood Market, rolling my cart down the produce aisle. I had mooched enough of Andrew's food; I figured it was time to chip in for some groceries. The least I could do was feed him.

It was hot out, though the brutal heat wave was gone. The sky was blinding blue, the wind summer-perfect. It was the kind of day that people took off work to go to beaches or parks, the kind of day to lounge in the shade before firing up the barbecue. I was wearing roomy cargo pants, a white tee, and flip-flops, my sunglasses pushed to the top of my head as I shopped. I paused my cart by the dairy case, stared blankly at a display of cheese, and realized I was happier than I could ever remember being in my life.

Seriously, I was so happy my feet felt like they were barely touching the floor. The past few days with Andrew had done that.

It wasn't just the sex—though, to be fair, the sex was amazing. Andrew had a brochure with twenty-six suggested positions in it, and we spent our nights experimenting with as many of them as possible. Some of them worked better than others, but it was always slow and hot and perfect. I'd never been with a man so focused on giving me pleasure, on getting it right, on making every time better than the last. It turned out I didn't need elaborate acrobatics or *Fifty Shades of Grey*. I just needed him. Only him.

But it honestly wasn't just the sex. Instead of sleeping afterward we usually talked, sometimes for hours, curled up and relaxed in the dark together. By day, we hung out, fully clothed, trading jokes and keeping each other company. Andrew was hard at work on the Lightning Man comics, and he had his appointments. Yesterday I'd met his psychotherapist, a fiftyish man named Dr. Costas who was very dignified and serious, though the crow's feet around his eyes crinkled warmly when he greeted Andrew, as if he liked him a lot. The crinkling crow's feet meant I approved of Dr. Costas, and I left them alone to do their session.

I was busy; I had lawyers' meetings about my inheritance and errands to run. I had to pick up my check for the modeling gig and my one and only paycheck from Miller's. I had started packing up some of the things in my grandmother's house to donate or sell. I was starting to think of the house as mine, pondering how I might make it look if I stayed there.

Because it looked like I was going to stay there, at least for the foreseeable future. I had no desire to leave Millwood, no wish to live anywhere except across the street from Andrew Mason. I'd picked up information for applying to nursing school. If they accepted me, I was going to do it, which would keep me here for at least the next few years.

For the first time in my life, things felt settled. They felt good. I didn't know where Andrew and I were going, but at the moment I sure as hell liked it. But I spent a lot of time at his house, eating the food from his kitchen. So here I was today, balancing that out.

I put fruit in my cart, and nuts and Greek yogurt. Andrew was a healthy eater, which was why he had such a hot body. He also worked out in his workout room every day, and I approved of the resulting muscles. Yum.

I turned the corner to the cereal aisle, and someone blocked my way. I looked up. It was a man—a handsome, pretty much gorgeous, man. He had tousled dark hair, stubble, and muscles for days under his dark gray tee. His low-slung jeans hid what was obviously a perfect body. His Converse sneakers were practically disintegrating. I looked back up to his face and saw that he was scowling at me.

I'd never seen this man before, but I recognized him as clearly as if I'd met him dozens of times. It was in the cheekbones, the eyes, and definitely in the scowl. This could be no one else but—

"Nick Mason?" I said.

He crossed his arms over his chest, which did interesting things to his biceps. He had a wedding ring on his left hand. There was no doubt that Nick Mason was objectively a very attractive man, though the entire package did nothing for me physically. Which was curious, because Nick's brother pressed every single one of my sex buttons.

"You're Tessa Hartigan," he said. His voice was different than Andrew's, deeper and more growly. Andrew's face was a little thinner than Nick's, more mature from what he'd been through. Nick didn't move out of my way. Instead he looked me up and down, his gaze disapproving. I felt like he'd caught me coming off a stripper stage wearing a thong instead of grocery shopping on a summer afternoon in my most comfortable clothes.

I bristled at that look, the way it assessed and dismissed me.

"I'd say it's nice to meet you," I said, meeting his gaze head-on, "but something tells me you disagree."

His expression went hard. "You're fucking right I disagree," he said. "I don't know who you are, and I don't care. You need to get out of Andrew's life. Now."

TWENTY-EIGHT

Tessa

NO. Oh, hell no. I might be stupidly happy and made soft by great sex, but I was still the toughest girl in Millwood, and I had no time for Mason brother intimidation tactics. "Thanks for the advice," I said drily to Nick. "Now get out of my way."

He didn't budge. "I don't think you're listening."

I pushed my cart against his jean-clad thighs, but he still didn't move. I pulled my cart back, then rammed it forward harder, hitting his legs. Did he think he could actually scare me?

He finally moved aside, and I moved on down the aisle. "See, this is why I like your brother better than you," I said. "He doesn't try to physically intimidate me. Guys who can walk are overrated."

He walked next to my shoulder, sticking to me like glue. "Are you making fun of him?"

"I'll mace anyone who makes fun of him," I replied, picking

up a box of Andrew's favorite whole-grain cereal. "Are we done here?"

"No. You need to get out of his life."

I obviously wasn't going to get rid of him, so I sighed. "Why? Do tell."

"Because you'll hurt him."

I turned the corner to the next aisle. "Considering you don't know me, that's a far-reaching assumption."

"Jesus, you even talk like him. Those big words."

"Which is strange, because apparently you're the writer of the duo. You could try articulating yourself beyond growly threats to strange women in grocery stores." I paused as a thought hit me. "Wait a minute. Why did you follow me to the grocery store? You know where I live." I stopped my cart and put a hand on my hip. "It's because if you came to my front door, Andrew would see you on his security camera. Right? You don't want him to know you talked to me."

A muscle in his jaw twitched, but he didn't deny it. I could feel the tension coming off him in waves. I was pissing him off, which pleased me. If he thought I would play the demure, sweet girl, he was wrong. I turned and pushed my cart again.

"I am not threatening you," he said after a minute. He was still walking at my shoulder as I shopped.

"Oh?" I said. "And what will happen if I don't get out of Andrew's life? You'll send me a strongly worded email?"

"Listen," Nick said. "You don't understand what you're dealing with here. You don't understand my brother."

"I understand him pretty well, actually." *Including how he kisses and his favorite sexual positions,* I thought. But I didn't say it, because it was none of Nick's business.

"Andrew isn't like other guys."

"That's why I like him."

"You still don't get it. He isn't just some Tinder dude you can date and then dump when you're bored. He doesn't play the dating game. If you dump him, you'll mess him up."

"And who says I'm going to dump him?"

Nick snorted. "So you're in this for a long-term relationship? You want to marry him?"

"It's none of your business what I want," I snapped. "Besides, maybe Andrew doesn't want a long-term relationship. Maybe he'll be the one to dump me."

I sounded snarky, but it was a cover. Andrew might want to dump me after a while. He was grumpy and independent and used to being on his own. Once the glow of sex wore off, would I just be in the way?

And then what? I was supposed to live across the street from the guy who caved my heart in? Because—I already knew it—I was attached. Andrew meant more to me than anyone else ever had. I didn't want to think about him dumping me.

"Does he know what you do for a living?" Nick asked as I put my groceries on the checkout belt.

Nick had Googled me, obviously. "Of course he does," I said. "And he likes it."

"I'll bet," Nick said.

I rolled my eyes. "Shame me if you want, but I happen to know you don't have a job, either. And you never have. You're even more useless than I am."

"You model lingerie for a living," he growled.

I didn't, actually. Not anymore. I wasn't going to take any more modeling gigs, even if they came my way, and sitting on the passenger seat of my car was the stack of papers I had to go through to apply for nursing school. I was going to do something useful, even if Andrew's brother—and mother—thought I was a tramp. "So what?" I said to Nick.

"If Andrew is going to find someone, then he needs to find someone nice," Nick said. "Someone who cares for him. Someone... I don't know, selfless and giving or something. Someone who will put him first."

I paid for the groceries and picked up my bags. Nick stepped forward to take some of them—so he wasn't completely without manners—but I snatched them out of his hands and walked away.

I was stung. No, more than that—I was hurt. I wasn't selfless and giving? I wasn't nice?

And in the back of my mind was a little voice: *He's right. Andrew deserves someone better than you.*

"Okay," Nick said as he followed me across the hot parking lot. "I shouldn't have shit on your choice of job."

"Fuck you," I said without looking back at him. "Some of us have to make a living, and we do it however we can."

"Fine. You're right. I know I can be an asshole. Believe it or not, I'm the nice brother."

"I can't believe someone actually married you."

"Neither can I."

That was kind of funny, but I was still mad. I beeped open my car and opened the hatchback, shoving grocery bags in. "Andrew told me about the suicide attempts," I said.

"Jesus Christ. He did?"

"Yes." In a way I could see why Nick was acting like a flu virus. He'd been with Andrew through all of the worst times and nearly lost him. If it were me who worried about Andrew day and night and some bra-model hussy came along, waving her boobs at him, I'd scratch her eyes out and I wouldn't think twice.

"He never talks to anyone about that," Nick said.

"I know. That's because he never talks to people. Which isn't exactly good for him, by the way."

"I know." Nick ran a hand through his hair. It was nice hair; it was a nice hand. Nick's wife probably had to wipe up her drool every time she looked at him, even though he was a jerk. "I'm trying to get him to come with me to the comics convention in Detroit, but he refuses to go."

I tossed in the last bag of groceries and looked at him. It was my turn to be surprised. "He didn't tell me about that."

"That's because he's being his dumbass self and won't even consider it. They want us as guests on a panel and to sign comics for readers. It would be fucking amazing, but he won't go."

I could see that. A convention venue, crowds, a hotel—Andrew would hate all of those things. Still, I thought it over. "He should go," I said.

"I agree, and so do his doctor and his therapist."

I felt my jaw drop. "You talk to his doctors?"

"What do you think?" Nick said. "We've been crossing paths for seven years. His physiotherapist and his wellness therapist, too. They don't tell me anything confidential, but we all know each other, and we all talk. Even though he's an asshole, he's still everyone's favorite patient. They'd walk over broken glass for him."

"Really?" I said. "So I'm not the only one. I've had a crush on him since day one. Like, bad."

Nick sighed. "It doesn't matter how fucked up he is, that's the effect Andrew has on people. I'm used to it. Everyone who gets to know him goes nuts for him. And he doesn't even notice, which makes it worse."

We had a moment of silent agreement, the first one we'd had since he accosted me in the store. Both of us stood there in the ugly parking lot, thinking about how one guy in a wheelchair made us both crazy in the best possible way. It was almost like Nick and I had something in common, like we could be friends.

And then he ruined it. "I have to look out for him," Nick said. "There's been no one else to do it since the accident. I want what's best for him, that's all."

My throat closed. Because what was best for Andrew probably wasn't me. He was right. I wasn't nice or sweet or understanding. I didn't know how to be with a man who had as many needs as Andrew did, the sharp and specific kind that you couldn't guess at. Hell, I'd never even had a long-term relationship with a man who had working legs and an average IQ. I was in over my head with Andrew.

I was that raw teenage girl again, the one who wasn't good enough. Not good enough for her parents or school or friends or boys. I wasn't going to get accepted to nursing school—that was a pipe dream. The truth was, I was a fucked-up girl who was no one. I was hot and sexy, and that was literally all I was.

Andrew needed someone he could lean on, someone who could actually help him with his shit. He didn't need me.

"I got it," I said, my voice choked.

Nick's eyes narrowed in alarm when he heard my voice. "Hey," he said.

"No, really. I got it." I slammed my hatchback shut. "I'm okay for your brother to get laid with, but I don't cut it anywhere else. I hear you. We're clear."

For the first time, he looked a little bit contrite. "I didn't really... That isn't what I meant."

I pulled my sunglasses from on top of my head and put them on. "Sure it is," I said. "We understand each other, don't we, Nick Mason? I know your type, and you know mine. Have a nice day."

I got in my car and drove off, leaving him standing there, alone.

TWENTY-NINE

Andrew

WHEN TESSA CAME to the door, I buzzed her in, barely glancing at the security feed. I was deep in a coding problem on the Lightning Man website, my earbuds in my ears, CCR playing on my iPhone. I wasn't in a bad mood for once. In fact, life almost seemed pretty freaking good.

I'd run reports on Lightning Man sales this morning, and downloads were up twenty percent over the previous month. We had fans writing in to the Gmail account I'd set up and a company interested in printing Lightning Man merchandise. Evie, who owned a bakery during the day, had taken a few evenings to set up an Instagram account for us, and we already had over five thousand followers. The hobby that Nick and I—a college dropout and his depressed, wheelchair-bound brother—had started in desperation was catching on.

We'd never planned on taking Lightning Man public at first. But we had, and people were reading it. It felt pretty good.

And then there was Tessa.

I'd never planned on her, either, but here she was. Those long legs and that blonde hair. The way she arched an eyebrow when I was being an ass and the way she threw her head back and laughed when one of my jokes caught her off-guard. She was either hanging out with me during the day or sending me caustic texts from wherever she happened to be. And at night, there was sex. Glorious, magical, incredible sex. How had I lived so long without sex? How had I lived so long without Tessa?

She came through the door as I pulled my earbuds out, her arms weighed down with groceries. Her big sunglasses were on, showing only her nice nose and her sexy mouth. "Hey," she said.

I looked at the bags. "You bought groceries?"

"Well, yeah." She walked into the kitchen. "I eat all of your food, Mason, in case you hadn't noticed."

"I hadn't noticed," I said, watching her walk through the doorway. Even in loose-fitting cargo pants, Tessa walking was a nice thing to watch. The nicest. "You don't have to do that, you know."

"I know," she said from the kitchen. "I'm trying not to be an asshole."

It was something in her voice, maybe. A slightly flat tone. I put my phone down and turned my chair so I wasn't facing my desk. "What's wrong?"

She was still in the kitchen, the cupboards banging. "Wrong?"

"Yes, wrong. As in not right."

She was silent for a long minute as the cupboards continued to bang, the fridge opened and closed. Then she came back out to the living room, empty-handed. She pulled the sunglasses from her face and leaned against the doorframe, looking at me.

"What?" I said.

She blinked and bit her lip, looking away.

"Tessa."

"What are we doing?" she asked. "You and me."

I frowned. "What do you mean, what are we doing?"

"Us," she said. "Whatever it is that we're doing together. I've never even had a steady boyfriend, did you know that? The longest I've ever dated someone has been a week."

Something went cold in the middle of my back, moving up the back of my neck.

"I've never even owned a cat," Tessa went on. "I got my GED by the skin of my teeth when I was twenty-one. All I own is a few garbage bags full of clothes and that's it."

The cold had traveled to the pit of my stomach. "Tessa, what are you saying?"

She looked at me. I'd never seen her look quite like that, like someone had stripped the skin off her and left her raw. Not even when she'd banged on my door and told me her deepest secret.

"I'm saying I don't think I can do this," she said. "I thought I could, but I can't. I'm not a strong enough person."

Now the cold was in the back of my throat. My hands were like ice on the arms of my chair.

Dumping me. She was dumping me.

Part of me had expected it. What was she doing with me, anyway? I'd never figured it out. I was used to people leaving. I was too much, I knew. I was too difficult. It was all too fucking hard.

And still it hit me in the chest like the slice of a blade.

Through the numbness working its way through me, something crossed my mind. She hadn't been like this this morning; she'd been flirty and relaxed when she left, her usual self. "Something happened," I managed to say. "While you were out. Something happened."

"I did some thinking, that's all," Tessa said, but she looked a little panicked. She was a terrible liar, at least with me. "I just... thought things over."

"No, you didn't." I put my hands in my lap. "You overthink everything, like I do, but that isn't what this is. Something happened that made you do this."

She shook her head.

And then it came to me. My brother, telling me I didn't know Tessa, that she could be anyone. Then quietly picking up his things and leaving, the argument over. "It was Nick, wasn't it? Nick got to you."

Panic again. "Andrew, no one got to me."

"Bullshit." The word came out harsh, like sandpaper. My brother. My fucking brother, the person I relied on most in the world. "You were fine this morning. You were fine last night. You were a strong enough person then."

She flinched, the expression moving over her beautiful face. Pain crossing her blue eyes. She may not have been good enough for L.A., but I had never seen a woman as beautiful as Tessa. "What are you suggesting we do, Andrew?" she said, her voice raw. "Are you suggesting we become boyfriend and girlfriend, when neither of us knows how that works? That we move in together, get married, have kids? Are you suggesting we follow the script? Neither of us knows how to read it."

"I don't follow a script, and neither do you." My own voice was rough with pain. In a way, she was right. We'd never be a normal couple, starting with the fact that I couldn't take her on dates. My own fucked-up failings. "We can make our own script. Both of us do that already. We make this, whatever it is—we make it what we want it to be. We make the rules ourselves, and fuck whoever doesn't agree with them."

"Great," she said. "And then something bad happens. You have a bad day, or I do. Or both of us. And when that happens, I'm going to say the wrong things and make you angry or hurt your feelings. And I won't know how to handle any of it or what to do. I won't know what you need or how to give it. I'll be clueless and stupid. And I'll fuck it up."

"You're doing it right now," I said. "What did you and Nick do? Meet up somewhere I couldn't see you? Talk about me like I'm a kid you share with your ex? Figure out what's best for me?"

She let out a little sound in the back of her throat, halfway between a moan of pain and a growl of frustration. She ran a hand through her hair and pulled away from the doorframe. "I have to go."

"You don't have to, you want to," I said. "Let's be clear on that at least, Tessa. You're leaving because you want to."

"I don't know what I want." She walked toward the door. "I've never known, Andrew, and you haven't cleared things up at all."

"You're welcome."

"I have to go," she said again, like it was something she was repeating to herself, and the door closed behind her.

I didn't have to turn on the security feed to know she was walking back across the street to her own house, going in and closing the door. Shutting me out.

I sat there for a long time, the silence ringing loudly in the room. Taking one breath. And then another.

I'd had Tessa. And then I'd lost her.

One breath, and then another.

When the car had hit the guardrail seven years ago, I should have been knocked out. In a world with even an inch of justice, I should have been unconscious on impact, out of it until I woke up in the hospital.

I wasn't. I was awake every minute as the paramedics came. Awake in the dark, unable to move, with Theo dead beside me in the driver's seat. In a way, even though seven years had passed, that darkness was the same darkness I saw every night after the sun went down.

For a short while, I hadn't faced that darkness alone. Those had been the best nights of my life. Tonight I'd be alone again.

On the table next to me, my phone buzzed. I closed my eyes, then opened them again and wheeled over to grab it. It was Nick, calling me. I swiped to cancel the call.

He called again. I cancelled the call again.

Before he could redial, I texted him. *Leave me the fuck alone,* I wrote. *We're done.*

Then I turned my phone off, turned back to my computer, and got back to work.

THIRTY

Tessa: Andrew?

   Tessa: Andrew??

   Tessa: Please, please talk to me. It's been three days.

   Tessa: Please??

   Tessa: Okay, if you won't talk, then I will. I have no one else to talk to, anyway. It's two o'clock in the morning and I can't sleep. I'm lying on my sofa, wide awake, thinking about you.

   Tessa: I guess that's stupid, right? You're not talking to me. I deserve it. Maybe you won't talk to me again, because I freaked out the other day. I panicked. And I fucked up, just like you said.

   Tessa: You were right, by the way. Nick talked to me. He tracked me to the grocery store so you wouldn't know. He told me I'm not good enough for you, and I believed him. Or, the girl I used to be believed him. She's gullible like that.

   Tessa: And you were right that we talked about you behind your back. Like you aren't a grown man who can have face-to-face conversations. So we both fucked that up.

   Tessa: You aren't talking to him either. I know because he found my number somehow and called me. He's beside himself.

He even went to your door and you wouldn't let him in. If you're not talking to me, you should at least talk to him. I've never heard a man so wrecked in my life.

Tessa: He loves you, by the way. A lot. I wish I had a brother who loved me like that. Or a sister. Any sibling, really. Seriously, Andrew. Talk to him.

Tessa: I miss you.

Tessa: I put in my nursing school application. It was lonely. I wished I had you with me.

Tessa: That sounds selfish, like it's all about me. Except it isn't. I want to do whatever you're doing, talk about whatever you want to talk about. I don't care what it is. Even if you want to yell at me. I just fucking miss you, you know? I fucking miss you.

Tessa: I made a mistake, and I know that. I'm sorry. But at the same time, that screwed-up girl lives inside me. I do my best to shut her up, but I don't think she'll ever be gone. She's part of who I am. Does that make sense? Does it even matter?

Tessa: You haven't blocked my number, so I'm holding on to that. Like maybe you're listening.

Tessa: I miss sex with you.

Tessa: And all of the other things.

Tessa: I miss everything.

Tessa: Okay, I'll shut up now. Good night.

THIRTY-ONE

Andrew

I THOUGHT it would be the worst thing. Being dumped by Tessa. Learning the entire thing was arranged by my brother. Watching him stamp out the first happiness I'd had in seven years, as if he couldn't take seeing me happy with anyone but him, even though he'd gotten married.

Being unable to stop any of it.

And it was bad. It was very fucking bad. But in the depths of the shittiness, with my phone on silent and the quiet deafening, something happened. My mind cleared, just a little. I didn't die. Instead, I started to think.

Not about them. About me.

"Your tones are muted today," Donna the wellness therapist said as she lit some incense. "You've turned off all of your computer monitors. Something is different."

I was in sweats. I hadn't bothered to shower today, though I'd worked out like a motherfucker. Working out made my brain inch toward clarity, at least until my muscles gave out. "Donna," I said, "do me a favor and level with me for once. No bullshit. Just truth."

She shook out the match she was holding and straightened, looking at me.

"Do you tell my mother what happens in these sessions?" I asked her.

"No," she said.

"Do you tell my brother? Anyone?" The image of Tessa and Nick discussing me had stuck in my mind, and I couldn't quite get past it.

But that didn't have to do with them. It had to do with me.

"No," Donna said.

"Why do you keep coming back here?" It sounded whiny, but I was actually curious. "Why do you show up and listen to my shit? Is it just for money?"

She blinked, and for once she gave it to me straight instead of talking about crystals or auras. "I like you," she said. "I never had a son. I look at you and I think, 'What if that was my boy?' If you were my boy, I'd come here and talk to you. So that's what I do." She sat in the chair across from me, a thoughtful look on her face. "Also, you're so clearly at war with yourself, and you're so close to getting past it. So very, very close. I just need to push you a little ways along."

I stared at her. This woman had more insight than doctors and therapists who had ten times her education. "Be honest," I said. "The problem isn't my chi or my aura or the crystals in my house. The problem is me."

She frowned. "That's not quite the right way to see it. You create the problem, yes. But you're also the solution. They're both you."

I closed my eyes.

"What happened?" she asked, not unkindly.

I gave her the truth in a harsh, sad summary. "My girlfriend dumped me."

"Is that so? Because the phone on the table behind you keeps lighting up, over and over. Like someone is trying to talk to you."

I kept my eyes closed. "She told me it's too hard."

"Well, it is hard," Donna said. "She's not wrong about that. When people come across something hard, sometimes their instinct is to run. And then sometimes they regret it afterward, but they don't know what to do."

"She'll do it again," I said.

"So you forgive her again, because it matters. She matters."

I took a breath. Tessa did matter. And I knew my phone was lighting up behind me. I'd read every one of her texts last night, watching them come in one by one. *I fucking miss you.* Jesus, I fucking missed her, too.

I thought about Tessa coming to my door that first time with her *Hi* cake, waving at the camera. "I'm not doing the same thing again," I said to Donna. "I'm not following the same old pattern."

"So do something different," Donna said. "Just do something. Because Andrew, I have to say, you've chosen to do nothing for the past seven years. And I'm asking you, how far do you think it's gotten you?"

I opened my eyes. "Jesus, Donna. How did you get so wise?"

She lifted an eyebrow. "You're not the only one who's lived life, you know. Some of the rest of us have lived it too. Now, let's discuss essential oils."

THIRTY-TWO

Tessa

"NO GIFTS," the woman sitting across from me said. "No poems or big gestures. And definitely, definitely nothing sappy."

I was talking, of all people, to Evie Bates. She had just married Nick Mason, but she'd kept her last name, because she was cool like that. She owned a bakery in downtown Millwood, and when I'd tracked her down in desperation, looking for advice, she agreed to have a coffee and a pastry with me.

Evie was pretty, with red hair tied up in a messy bun. She was wearing a white tee under denim overalls, which actually looked hot on her—not an easy look to pull off. She wore very little makeup, but her skin glowed. Obviously Nick Mason, jerk that he was, could keep a woman pretty happy when he put his mind to it. And he had.

I wondered what she saw when she looked at me. I was wearing jeans, a black tee, and my big sunglasses, which I'd pushed up on my head. I'd left off the makeup and I definitely didn't look happy. I didn't care if she pitied me; I just wanted help.

"I don't envy you," she said. "Having a Mason brother unhappy with you isn't fun. Most women can't handle them even when they're in a good mood."

I slumped in my chair and put another bite of chocolate muffin in my mouth. It was freaking delicious. It was a novel feeling, being able to eat a chocolate muffin without worrying I'd have to strip later. If I could eat my feelings, then hell, I was going to. "So I guess another *Hi* cake is out of the question."

"Another what?"

"I bought him a cake that said *Hi* on it when I wanted to introduce myself."

Evie blinked at that, her big eyes widening. "And what did he do?"

I shrugged and put another piece of muffin in my mouth. "He didn't want it at first, but he took it. And he ate it."

Her jaw dropped. "Oh, my God."

"What?"

"He's in love with you."

I nearly choked on my bite of muffin. "What? Because he ate cake? Everyone likes cake."

"Are you kidding me? Look around." She gestured to the bakery we were sitting in, which was piled with amazing desserts. "This is a freaking *bakery*. I've been giving him baked goods for years. He never eats them. I finally had to stop doing it, because he was throwing them out. When his other neighbors gave him welcome presents, he left them in the garbage can at the end of the driveway."

I had to admit that was promising, but still. "I was pretty pathetic. Maybe he just felt sorry for me."

Evie looked uncertain. "I guess it's possible, but Tessa, this is Andrew. Being sorry for people isn't exactly his specialty."

"He didn't know me then, though. And even when I stayed with him during the heat wave—"

"You what?"

She really seemed shocked, so I explained. "It was a heat wave, and my air conditioning was broken. He let me stay at his house and—"

"At his *house*?" She couldn't do anything but repeat my words back to me, louder and louder. "He let you *stay* at his *house*?"

"I guess you didn't know that, because you were on your honeymoon at the time. It was really nice of him. He insisted I take the bedroom, and he slept on the couch." I felt my cheeks go hot, because those were the days before we shared the bedroom. That had been raw and life-changing and fun. I wanted it back, really bad—but I wasn't about to share that with his sister-in-law.

Evie didn't notice me squirming, because she'd dropped her head into her hands. "Oh, my God. This is a disaster. He's never had anyone in his house, Tessa. Even Nick has never slept there. I didn't know he was so nuts about you. I just thought..."

When she trailed off, I added helpfully, "You thought I was just a hot girl he was fucking, and that I was probably using him for something or other."

"No! No." She sat up again. "I didn't think that. I have my own past, and so does Nick, okay? We don't judge. I just thought —we just thought—it was casual. Andrew doesn't have relationships."

I brushed muffin crumbs from my hands. "Well, you can relax, because he doesn't have a relationship now. Even though I keep trying to get him back."

She looked at me, coming to some kind of decision. "You have to get him back. You have to."

"I know that," I said. "That's why I'm here."

"Well, you're right. You have to get him back. He's in love with you, and you broke it off."

"I'm in love with him, too," I said, because it was so obviously true, there was no point in pretending it wasn't.

"I just hope he's okay," she said. "What's been going on at the house?"

"The wellness therapist came yesterday." It was funny—I was the one watching Andrew's house now, instead of him watching mine. "The landscapers came yesterday afternoon. This morning someone I didn't recognize came. A woman."

"A woman?" Evie said. "Not the housekeepers?"

"No, a solo woman." I pressed my lips together. The woman, whoever she was, had been in her mid-twenties and pretty, carrying a bag over her shoulder. She'd been in Andrew's house for an hour, which I knew because I'd watched for her to come out. What pretty twenty-five-year-old came to Andrew's house for an hour? He'd never told me anything about that. Who was she, and what was she doing with him?

Evie looked as confused as I was. "I don't know who that is," she said. "It isn't on the schedule."

"I know." I knew the schedule, too. Maybe even better than she did. "Whoever she was, she probably thought he was hot. Damn it."

"We can fix this," Evie said. "We need to get you two face to face, that's all. Let him see you in person and talk it out."

"Well, since Andrew doesn't leave his house, that means I have to get in. Which he won't allow."

Evie reached across the table and patted my hand. "We'll think of something, I promise."

THIRTY-THREE

Tessa

EVIE and I didn't have to think of something clever or nefarious, it turned out. Because in the end, Andrew did the unthinkable.

He left his house.

I came home from dropping off a load of my grandmother's old things to charity when I saw the handmade signs taped to the streetlights and stop signs on the street. *Neighborhood BBQ! Games! Music! Starts at 4 PM!* It was almost 4:30, and I could hear the sound of music and laughter coming from the park at the end of the street, wafting on the smell of cooking hamburgers.

I hesitated, glancing at Andrew's house. It was the perfect excuse; I should go over there and knock on his door, wave at the security camera, ask him to go with me. Except he wouldn't—I already knew that. He wouldn't go with anyone, and definitely not with me.

Still, I was lonely, and the neighbor women I'd met on my first day here were nice. I didn't feel like sitting alone in my grandmother's house, thinking about Andrew, even though the air conditioning was working now. It sounded too pathetic. So I put my keys in my pocket and followed the signs down the street.

The music and voices got louder, the barbecue smells stronger. It was a beautiful day, hot and breezy. I was almost at the park when Amy, one of the neighbor women, noticed me and came down the walk toward me. "Tessa!" she called out. "You came! Welcome to the neighborhood party!"

"Thanks," I said, smiling at her. I'd come a long way from L.A., but I realized I didn't mind.

"Let me grab you a drink." She led me to the edge of the park, to a little spot under some trees where there was a line of coolers. "Jan, this is Tessa, remember?" I waved at Jan, who was standing over one of the coolers holding a plastic glass filled with white wine. The two women looked at each other while Amy poured me a glass. "It's so exciting," Jan said. "Did you see?"

"See what?" I sipped my wine. It was cheap white wine from a cooler, drunk from a plastic cup, but somehow it was delicious. "What's going on?"

"Your neighbor," Amy said. "Andrew Mason. He's *here*."

I lowered my glass and stared at her. "Andrew is here?"

"You're on a first-name basis?" Jan said, her eyes wide. "Do tell."

"Oh, my God." I turned and looked at the crowd, which was a few dozen strong. Sure enough, on the other side of the park, I could see Andrew's wheelchair. He had his back to me, and he was in the shadow of one of the big trees. A little boy was talking to him, gesturing excitedly about something.

He was here. Andrew was here. No one had asked him or coerced him. He just came.

I knew him. I knew how he was, how he hated gatherings like this. How he hated leaving his house at all. Why had he come?

"He's so funny," Amy said, gushing. "And so smart. He isn't

an asshole at all. Did you know he draws comics? My kids have gone nuts for him. My son thinks he's actually Batman."

"Plus he's gorgeous," Jan said.

"I know." I watched as the boy said something to Andrew, Andrew replied, and the boy ran off, excited.

"She found a way to meet him already," Jan said. "I knew it. Amy, you owe me ten bucks."

But her voice was behind me, because I was walking across the park toward Andrew. I picked up a lawn chair from a stack leaning against a tree and carried it with me, downing the last of my plastic glass of wine. *Now or never, Tessa.*

Andrew didn't turn as I approached, but the line of his shoulders tightened. Just a little. I noticed.

I unfolded my chair next to his and sat down. He was wearing jeans and a navy blue tee, a plaid navy flannel unbuttoned over it. He had a plastic cup of beer in his hand. His beard was trimmed all the way down, almost to stubble, and he'd had a haircut. He glanced at me, just the briefest look from his dark eyes. "Tessa," he said.

I swallowed and tried to find a spine. Tried to think of something to say. "What did you say to that kid?" I finally asked.

Andrew glanced at me again, and I stared at the line of his throat where it disappeared into the neck of his tee. "I told him that Lightning Man is real, he's my friend, and he's watching him, especially on Halloween," he said.

I felt myself smiling. "That's very devious, Andrew."

He shrugged. "Someone has to teach kids manners. It may as well be Lightning Man."

Everything hung in the air around us—everything important and unsaid. "You're drinking a beer," I said.

"I'm sipping a beer," he corrected me. "Apparently you can't come to one of these things without drinking something.

Everyone insisted." He looked at his cup. "It's piss warm, but if I get rid of it, someone will just give me another."

"Well," I said, my throat tight, "I'm glad you're here at all."

He looked at me then—not just a glance, but a look. There were so many things in that look: anger, fear, raw hurt. There was the humor and the strength he carried with him all the time. And he was glad to see me; I could see that, too. I could see that my presence made things better for him, just like his did for me, even if he didn't want it to. I could see that I was making this whole situation easier for him, just by sitting next to him in this lawn chair, feeling the breeze on my face and commiserating about his warm beer.

I wanted to sit next to him like this in every situation, make him feel better every day. Just like he did for me.

"Aren't you going to ask me why I came here?" he asked me.

"Okay," I said. "Why?"

"Because I thought it was time."

I bit my lip and nodded. I had a lump in my throat.

"Also, I wanted to impress you."

That made me laugh. "Andrew, you always impress me."

"With my remarkably bad humor and my shitty life, yes."

"And your sexual skills."

"Those too, of course. But I wanted to impress you some other way for once."

I was nearly sagging in my lawn chair. This was the Andrew I knew, witty and tough and funny. I was so glad to see him. But I kept up the conversation, because I knew the last thing he wanted was to see me get sappy. "Well, it worked. I am impressed. So are the neighbors. You've won them over, especially the women."

"They're curious about me," he said with a dismissive wave. "One old lady talked to me at top volume, as if being in a wheelchair means I'm hard of hearing. Another guy said 'I'm sorry, dude,' at least four times. I had to call Bea Arthur on both of them."

I laughed again. "Did you actually say 'Bea Arthur?'"

"I did. It was singularly ineffective. Now my neighbors think I'm an avid *Golden Girls* fan instead of the dignified intellectual I really am."

I leaned back in my chair, my eyes watering with laughter. "Oh my God, you are so badass."

"Obviously," Andrew said. He ran a hand through his hair. "You know, I don't know what I was avoiding all this time. Except for the yelling lady and the sorry dude, it isn't all that bad."

I watched his gorgeous hand as it moved through his hair, wishing avidly that hand was on my skin instead. Then I remembered that his hair was shorter than it was a few days ago. "A haircut!" I said, sitting up straight in my lawn chair. "That girl who came to your house gave you a haircut!"

Andrew frowned at me. "Well, sure. Wait a minute —what girl?"

"The good-looking one I watched from my window."

"You watched Candy from your window?"

"Her name is *Candy*?" I thumped my palm against the arm of my chair. "For real? No one is named Candy. Plus she's younger than me, and her boobs were almost as nice as mine. I'm going to have to kill her."

"Tessa."

"Now I'm going to have to go to haircutting school as well as nursing school. Damn it."

He rolled his eyes. "I didn't see Candy's boobs, okay? She cut my hair, that's all." Politely he added, "Though from what I could see, they weren't as nice as yours at all."

Just like that, the air went heavy between us. We were talking about sex, about us, and yet we weren't at all. This was just how we did things, two people as damaged as we were. This was how we understood each other. And we did.

I said, "You read my texts." It wasn't a question.

Andrew looked away for a minute, his shoulders tensing again. "Yeah, I did."

"I meant them," I said. "I'm sorry for what I said. For freaking out and leaving." I swallowed. "I'm just really, really sorry. Can we go back?"

He was quiet for a minute as the music and the voices washed around us, like white noise. I couldn't have said who a single person was in this park right now. Just Andrew Mason. That was all.

"There's no going back," he said finally. He turned and looked at me, his dark eyes finding mine. "There's only forward."

My heart skipped a beat in hope. "Okay."

He shook his head. "You have to be sure. Are you? Is that what you really want?"

"Yes."

"Tessa. You said it's hard, and you were right. This shit is *hard*. I'm fucked up, deeply and permanently. You have an idea of how much."

"Fuck that," I said, my voice rough. "You put every other man I've met to shame. You're a thousand times the man they are. And in case you haven't figured it out, I'm completely in love with you." I took a breath. "So, yes, it's hard, but I can do it. *We* can do it. We'll just have to make our own script, right?"

He was watching my face, his gaze traveling the line of my jaw, the curve of my cheek, then meeting my eyes. "That's the idea," he said softly.

I held his gaze with mine. "Then I'm in."

A smile touched the corner of his mouth, and my heart skipped another beat.

"Okay then," Andrew said. "We may as well scandalize the neighborhood."

He leaned over, cupped the back of my head in one hand, and kissed me.

Right there where everyone could see.

I kissed him back, leaning in. He tasted like Andrew and summer and a little like warm beer. It was the best flavor in the world.

We kissed like that for a long time, until a kid laughed and a few of the adults whistled.

Then we kept going.

And eventually, we ditched our drinks and he took me home.

THIRTY-FOUR

Andrew

One month later

"I THINK this is the stupidest thing I've ever done," I said.

"No," my brother said. "That was when you jumped off the roof when you were nine."

"I was Superman," I said. "Besides, my ankle only broke a little."

Nick opened the passenger door of his car. "It broke a lot. Your foot was practically twisted the wrong way. I was traumatized."

"You always were a bit of a chicken."

He glared at me. "Jesus Christ. Just get in."

I wheeled up to the door and put my brake on. I pulled

myself out and into the car, putting myself in the passenger seat. Trying not to puke or pass out, or both.

"Take it easy on him," Evie said to her husband as he collapsed my chair and put it in the back of the car. "This is a big deal. Andrew, are you okay?"

My vision was swimming. "I'm fine," I managed, my mouth dry.

"Do you need drugs?" Nick asked.

I shook my head. A Xanax high was a pretty tempting way to get through the drive to the comics convention, but I wanted to keep my head clear.

I was actually doing this. Going to a convention in Detroit, talking on a panel with Nick, then staying in a hotel overnight and coming home tomorrow. How the hell had I agreed to this again?

Oh, right. Tessa.

Tessa could talk me into anything. One minute I was bantering with her like we always did, and the next thing I knew I was agreeing to some fucked-up idea. She was like magic. She didn't even have to take her clothes off.

That was what happened when you were in love with someone.

Yes, me. In love. Who the hell said this story could have a happy ending? I could say I was surprised, but then again, this was Tessa we were talking about. Falling in love with her was as easy as breathing, even for someone like me.

Making it work was harder, but there was nothing I would rather do.

She wasn't coming with us—she had an important orientation session today at the nursing school she'd been accepted into. Classes started in three days, and she was so excited and nervous that she was probably sitting in the session right now, panicking just like I was. Both of us were doing entirely different things, yet feeling exactly the same wave of anxiety. It was weirdly comforting in a way.

Evie got in the back seat, and Nick started the car. He glanced at me, I gave him the thumbs-up, and we started.

I felt different than I had a month ago, even though on the surface a lot of things were the same. I still lived in my house, and Tessa still lived in hers. We weren't ready for anything else yet, especially since most of my house was custom fitted for me. But I'd given Tessa my security code so she could come and go whenever she wanted. Her girly things were in my bathroom. And she'd called a contractor to put a ramp on her porch so I could go to her place, too.

And sometimes we went out. There were a few restaurants and coffee shops in Millwood that could accommodate a wheelchair. We went to the movies and the park. It wasn't always simple and it was sometimes exhausting, but I'd finally learned the most important thing: Even after you've lived through something as bad as I had, you had to live your fucking life. As in, stop just existing and actually live it.

It was hard sometimes, but when was anything worth doing easy?

I'd started going out to my appointments instead of making people come to me. I visited Dr. Arnaud at his office, and I visited my therapist, too. I still made Jon come to me for physio, because I liked to make him work. I also had Donna the wellness therapist come, too, though not as often. She said that my energies were so improved that I barely needed her help anymore.

Sometimes it was Tessa who took me to appointments, and sometimes it was Nick. My brother and I had patched things up after he apologized. I made him apologize to Tessa, too, which he did. And then, as usual, we were fine. Nick and I were blood; he was my other half. There was almost nothing I wouldn't forgive him for; this one was easy. We went back to making comics, Nick on my sofa with Scout on his lap while I drew.

Life was actually good, which was probably why I got fooled into agreeing to this crazy trip.

I was lightheaded as soon as we hit the highway. My hand gripped the door handle, my knuckles white. It had been seven years, but being on the highway sent me back to that night, the way we spun toward the guardrail, the darkness. Theo dying next to me. The sirens far in the distance as I waited.

But that was over. It was in the past. I was still alive, and I would be for a long time. I had things to do, a life to live. A woman to love. This wasn't going to get the best of me—not this time.

"Music?" Nick asked. He was staying quiet, reading my mind. Evie was quiet, too. I nodded and Nick turned on the music on his iPhone. Beautiful music filled the car, and then a beautiful voice: Roy Orbison singing "Mystery Girl." I unclenched my hands, relaxed into the car seat, and smiled.

"What?" Nick said.

"You're a romantic," I said, loud enough for his wife to hear in the back.

"Shut up, dickhead," Nick said, but he was smiling, too.

WHEN YOU MAKE comics in your suburban living room, you forget that real people are reading them. The download numbers are just figures on a screen, not real people. It's easy to pretend that there are no real people somewhere past your door, reading the thing you work so hard on.

But it hit home when Nick and I came onto the stage at the convention. The lights overhead were bright, but I could still see that there were over a hundred people in the audience, waiting to see us. Us. The Mason brothers, who had started spinning stories in my hospital room because it was better than pain. Who the hell wanted to see us?

The moderator introduced us, and we waved. The room applauded. They had put a table on the stage with three microphones, one for the moderator and two for us. The moderator was going to ask us questions, and then we were going to take questions from the audience.

My mouth was dry. Cold sweat coated my back. I had no idea if I would be able to say anything at all. And then I looked out at the audience, and Tessa was there.

She was sitting right in the front row. She was wearing jeans and a zip-up hoodie with the name of her nursing school on it, sneakers on her feet. She was the most beautiful woman in the room—her flawless skin, her blonde hair, her gorgeous blue eyes. Those eyes were fixed on me, and she was smiling.

She'd made it.

I smiled back at her, and everything fell away. There was just Tessa and me. That was always how it was with us: Wherever we were, there was just her and me. I tended to forget that anyone else was in the room, and so did she.

The moderator finished his introductions and was about to start his first question when I leaned toward my microphone and said, "I just want to clear something up before we start, because we get a lot of questions. Let's just make this clear. Lightning Man and Judy Gravity are dating."

The room erupted—applause, shouts of protest. There was a big divide among Lightning Man fans about the state of the Lightning Man-Judy Gravity romance. It was by far the topic of the most emails we got.

I looked at Tessa again. She was cheering, of course.

"This is going to be a lively debate," the moderator said. "What's your opinion, Nick?"

Nick had noticed Tessa, too. Probably because she was sitting right next to Evie, who was also clapping. "Lightning Man," he said, "is definitely dating Judy Gravity. No question."

Over the roar of the audience, I watched Tessa laugh.

And I knew, for the first time, that everything was going to be okay.

EXCERPT FROM SPITE CLUB

Evie

It started with a phone call at one o'clock in the morning.

I'd put my pillow over my head to block out my roommate's music, and I pulled my head out when I heard the ringtone, my hair falling over my eyes as I reached for my phone. I didn't recognize the number. "Hello?"

A strange man's voice on the other end said, "Evie Bates?"

"Yes?" I croaked, half into my pillow in my dark bedroom.

"Is your boyfriend a guy named Josh Brantwell?"

"Yes." I sat bolt upright, shoving my hair back. "Oh my God, is he okay?"

"Not for long."

The man's voice was rough, as if he'd been shouting over a bar band all night, and I could hear the faint sounds of street noise in the background. I had never heard that voice before, and for a second I got a strange chill down my spine, like a premonition of doom.

"What?" I said. "What are you talking about?"

There was a pause. Then the man's voice came again, dark and cold. "Look, Evie Bates, I realize this is probably bad news, but I'm about to go beat your boyfriend to a pulp."

For a second, the words didn't compute. "Who is this?" I nearly shouted, standing up in the dark in my old pajama top.

"It's going to be bloody. I just thought I should warn you first."

"Is this a joke?" It didn't sound like a joke. It sounded like someone was about to beat up Josh. Was he being mugged? No, muggers didn't phone their victims' girlfriends first. And Josh couldn't get mugged unless he was out on the street somewhere, when I knew exactly where he was. He was—

"No joke," the strange man said. "My girlfriend is at Josh Brantwell's place right now. And I'm about to go mess him up."

That stopped me. It made no sense. "There's no girl at Josh's place," I said stupidly. "He's there alone."

"You sure about that?" the man said. "Because I followed my girlfriend tonight. And she came here." He rhymed off an address that made my stomach drop to the floor. "Resident is one Josh Brantwell."

"What is she doing there?" I said.

"Fucking him, I presume," the man said bluntly. "I'm pretty pissed off about it, I have to say. I'm about to go in there and give him a beating. But I looked him up first, and I saw that he has a girlfriend. So hey, Evie Bates, your asshole of a boyfriend is cheating on you. I thought you should know."

"I—" I couldn't think, couldn't speak. Josh? "I—"

"Well?" the man said.

"I have no idea what you're talking about."

"Yeah," the man said. "I thought so. Bring bandages, a towel, maybe a mop." Then he hung up.

For a second I stared at the wall of my bedroom, my mouth open.

Then I grabbed my clothes.

There was no way Josh was cheating on me. Simply no way. There had to be a mistake somewhere.

We'd been dating for four months. I met him at the bank where we were both tellers. He was dark-haired, clean-cut, good-looking, and when he asked me out I said yes. Of course I did. Josh was the Yeti of boyfriends: straight, single, sober, no baggage. I was twenty-five, and I was *supposed* to have a boyfriend like that. It was flattering that he'd picked me, when the other single women at work were circling him like sharks. I hadn't asked a lot of questions—I'd just gone on the date.

And it was going well. We got along. We liked the same TV shows. The sex was normal and semi-regular. I'd met his family, and he'd met my mother, who had pulled me aside and told me in a low voice that she could *see a future for me with a young man like that.* Finally, finally, I was putting in place everything I needed: a good job, a nice boyfriend, a regular life, my mother's approval. It was finally happening.

The call could be a fake. Maybe this guy—I had no idea who he was—was just crazy. Maybe he was a serial killer, trying to lure me to my death. But I thought about the voice I'd heard on the phone, rough and a little dangerous, and I felt that chill again. The stranger hadn't sounded like a serial killer. He'd sounded honest and very, very pissed off.

Still, I told myself there was a mistake somewhere. The stranger's cheating girlfriend had gone to a different address, not Josh's. Or something. Because Josh was definitely, definitely not cheating.

Right?

I gripped the wheel and pulled up to Josh's condo complex

and thought about signs. Were there signs when a guy was cheating? What were they supposed to be? We didn't have sex often, but then we never had. That was what happened when you were in a regular relationship, I'd told myself calmly. That was real life. No one went around having sex all the time, anyway. You did it on a schedule, when you were free and you were both in the mood. Had we been having sex even less than usual? When was the last time? I stared at the door of his building and thought back. Saturday night? No, he'd gone out with his friends. It must have been before that.

How else was I supposed to know he was cheating? We didn't fight. He got a lot of attention from female coworkers and customers at work, but he didn't make a big deal about that. He didn't act furtive, and I hadn't caught him lying. In fact, I'd been starting to think about having the Big Conversation with him. The one about Us and Our Future and Maybe Moving In. I had a schedule. I *needed* a schedule. Without a schedule, I would mess everything up. I was determined not to mess up this time. I was determined to make it work.

Bring bandages, a towel, maybe a mop.

I got that chill of premonition again.

No. Just no. I was going to handle this. And everything would be fine.

It was raining, a warm June rain. We'd just come off of a cold, shitty Michigan winter, and even the rain was welcome after the months of snow. I got out of the car and walked up Josh's driveway, letting myself get wet. Josh lived in a complex of townhouse condos, attached in a long line like one of those cutout crafts you did in public school. The complex was brand new. It was his first place, bought with his nice bank salary. In every way, my boyfriend was on the way up.

There was a second car in the driveway, parked behind Josh's treasured Mustang. A pretty little car, as red as lipstick. And beyond that, parked on the street, was another black car I didn't recognize, inky in the darkness.

There was no one around. This was a neighborhood of nice young professionals, tidy and brand new, unlike the rest of Millwood, Michigan. This wasn't where the drunks and the teenagers and the pot dealers hung out. This was where people had jobs they had to get up for in the morning, and they all went to bed at ten.

There were lights on in Josh's place. An upstairs light, and a light downstairs in the living room. More ominously, the front door was open. Just a little—it was a few inches ajar—but it was open. And something was going on inside. A man was bellowing. A woman was shouting. There was a thump, a crash of something breaking.

Oh, shit.

I ran the rest of the way up the driveway. A neighboring door opened, and a woman of about thirty-five stepped on to her porch, giving me a total bitch face that could turn you into stone from twenty feet away. "I'm about to call the cops!" she shouted at me. "See if I don't! I can hear them straight through the connecting wall!"

"Don't do it!" I shouted back. I ran past her to Josh's doorway.

Inside, the living room was carnage. Josh's nice Ikea coffee table was overturned, and one of the brand-new blinds had been ripped from the living room window—it hung crazily, making the whole room look like it was on an angle.

Josh was lying on the floor, curled up in pain, his hands over his face. Blood seeped through his fingers. He was wearing nothing but a pair of tighty whities, his gym-toned body on display. Standing next to him, shouting *Stop*, was a woman with long, dark curly hair. She was gorgeous and sexy, and she was wearing a t-shirt I recognized as Josh's, and obviously nothing else. I could literally see her bare ass.

That answered the cheating question, then.

Something inside me snapped, and I went numb. I stopped seeing Josh's nice living room, where we'd watched TV and made out with his hand down my pants. I stopped seeing the nice furniture, some of which I'd helped him pick out. I stopped seeing his nice body, that I'd had sex with on a nice regular schedule for four nice months. I stopped seeing anything at all except that woman's bare ass, perfectly round and much smaller than mine, beneath the hem of my boyfriend's T-shirt.

Was that feeling heartbreak? I didn't know. Embarrassment? Pain? Maybe it was just the feeling of all of your life's plans flushing down the toilet in a single second.

Then I noticed the man.

Standing over Josh, looking down at him, was a guy I didn't know. He was wearing beat-up jeans, motorcycle boots—one of which was untied—and a gray T-shirt so worn that the hem had come unstitched. A brown leather jacket lay discarded on the floor at his feet. His hands were curled into fists, his arms flexed. They were impressive arms, sleek with muscle. In fact, all of him was impressive—his shoulders, his back through the thin shirt, his narrow waist. He had tousled brown hair, a scruff of stubble, a face that knocked me back. My first thought was *Jesus, he's good-looking.* Everyone in this little scene was good-looking except, maybe, me. And they were all so focused that not a single one of them had noticed me.

"Hey," I said.

Everyone turned and looked at me. It was like a crazy tableau, and for a second it hurt so sickeningly much that I felt like laughing. *Evie Finds Boyfriend With Pants Down.* I was breathless with pain, but I was also a little detached. *Is this really happening? Why can't I feel anything? What's wrong with me?*

Josh dropped his hands from his face, and I could see blood dripping from his nose. *"Evie!"* he said, in a tone of such pure horror it was almost comical. I felt like laughing again. Or maybe screaming.

The bare-assed woman took her turn. "Oh, my God!" she cried, dropping to her knees. "Josh!" She touched him gingerly, getting close to but not quite touching any blood. She looked up at the man above her. "Stop hitting him, Nick, you asshole!"

But Nick, the asshole, wasn't even looking at her. He was looking at me.

He was still poised in his fight stance, his fists curled, but instead of looking angry or threatening, he looked... distracted. His gaze took me in, up and down, and then it rested on my face, his eyes catching mine, as if he was trying to figure something out.

I was wearing a green T-shirt and denim overalls. Okay, fine, overalls aren't exactly fashionable, but they were the first things I pulled off the floor. The overalls, plus the gray cardigan I'd put on, hid the fact that I wore no bra, so that was a win. May in Michigan, especially in the middle of the night, is not exactly warm, and my nipples were showing the fact behind the overalls. I had flip-flops on my feet—my toes were wet and freezing—and my shoulder-length hair was a mess, my face devoid of makeup and probably creased with sleep. I wasn't exactly Giselle, but at least my ass was covered.

"Evie," Josh said from the floor. "I can explain."

"Nick, he's bleeding!" the beautiful woman shrieked. "Should we call an ambulance? What do we do?"

"No ambulance!" Josh replied. He rolled over and groaned, cupping his bleeding nose. The only person who didn't say anything was Nick, who was still looking at me.

Despite the craziness of the scene, and my hurt, and the fact that my boyfriend had—it seemed likely—recently put his dick into the bare-assed girl, I was calm. *Be polite,* my mother had always taught me. *No one likes a girl who makes a fuss.* That's who I was now. I was the polite girl, after years of failure at it. I ran a hand through my hair, thinking maybe I *should* make a fuss in this situation—but then again, Josh and the gorgeous woman were making enough of a fuss for everyone.

I met Nick's gaze without flinching. I couldn't read his expression.

"The neighbors are about to call the cops," I told him in my oddly normal voice.

He blinked once—his eyelashes were ridiculously dark—and looked down at Josh, who was still moaning. I watched him uncurl his fists. He toed Josh with his boot, nudging him in the ribs as the woman poked at him, still not getting bloody. "Hey," he said, the voice I recognized from the phone call. "Shut up."

The woman wasn't done. "You asshole!" she shouted at Nick again.

Nick actually sighed. "You shut up, too, Gina," he said. She went quiet, still glaring.

I should be screaming, or crying maybe. I should be losing my shit. Instead, I watched as Nick bent and picked up his brown leather jacket, shrugged it on. He scrubbed a hand over his face. His knuckles were red—he'd given Josh a hell of a hit. There was a second of furious satisfaction at that, and then I pushed it down again. That wasn't me.

Ignoring the two on the floor, Nick walked toward me, his untied boot clomping loudly. I felt a jolt of alarm low in my belly. I'd met bad boys in my life—even done things I shouldn't with a few of them, back when I was Old Evie—but I'd never seen one like this. This Nick guy owned a room without even trying. He probably wrecked things without even trying, too. Lives. Women. Virginities. Reputations. He was that kind of guy.

Still, I assumed that with his ass-kicking finished he would leave, and Old Evie felt a pang over it. I didn't know who Nick was, but he was very fucking cool, and I envied him that. Old

Evie would have followed a guy like this like a lapdog. "Thanks for the phone call," I said to him.

He stopped, looking at me again in that way he had, like he was figuring something out. "Yeah?"

"I mean it." I did. If he hadn't called me, I would have continued getting cheated on, not knowing about it. It wasn't his fault. "It takes guts to be the bearer of bad news."

Nick considered that, his gorgeous gray eyes looking me over. "Are you pissed off, Evie Bates?" he asked in his bar-band growl.

It was a strange question, but somehow it fit the strange, surreal night I was having. I looked past him at Josh and naked girl, who were watching us. Josh had sat up, and I could see his nicely styled hair, his washboard stomach. He'd had sex with me a week ago, on my bed in my apartment. I remembered now.

Old Evie would have screamed at Josh. New Evie didn't make a fuss.

But maybe both Evies were angry.

I nodded, answering Nick's question. "Yeah. I think I'm pissed off."

"Yeah?" Nick said. "Okay, then. You hungry?"

Another weird question, but suddenly I was. I really fucking was. It was like he was hypnotizing me. I shouldn't do this, not even a little. I should tell him to take a hike.

I should go home and get back in bed and pull up the covers and handle this like an adult. I should get some sleep so I'd be ready for work in a few hours. I should be rational and work through it and partake in self-care and do whatever you were supposed to do when your boyfriend cheated on you. I should work on getting past this and healing. I should get through this and come out better and stronger than before. Giving in to base instincts was not going to help with any of that.

I looked at Nick. It was two in the morning. I was pissed. And he was ridiculously hot.

Bad idea, Evie.

Shut up, Old Evie said.

"I'm starving," I told Nick.

He nodded back. It was like he understood everything.

"Me too," he said. "Let's go."

ALSO BY JULIE KRISS

The Riggs Brothers Series

Drive Me Wild

Take Me Down

Work Me Up

Make Me Beg

The Bad Billionaire Series

Bad Billionaire

Dirty Sweet Wild

Rich Dirty Dangerous

Back in Black

Mason Brothers

Spite Club

The Eden Hills Duet

Bad Boyfriend

Bad Wedding